PRETENDING IN PARADISE

FRANKY BROWN

Pink

PALMETTO
PRESS

Contents

Prologue

Lily

My cousin Amy had excellent taste. Her wedding at her family's church in North Las Vegas was beautiful, and the reception in a ballroom at the Bellagio hotel on the Vegas strip was going perfectly. Shining gold chandeliers hung from the ornate ceiling, a DJ was set up with large speakers on an elevated stage with red velvet curtains behind him. The room floor featured a Persian rug in a blue, red, and yellow paisley pattern.

The ballroom was filled with pink and white flowers on every surface. It had a large open area for dancing and was surrounded by round tables with white tablecloths. Tall vases with red roses were at the center of each.

The place settings were elegantly simple and the wedding cake was decorated with a delicately piped basket weave and sprinkled with pink rose petals.

I thought this would be me.

I thought I was going to marry my boyfriend Alex and live happily ever after. As it turned out, he didn't share my thoughts.

Our cousin Amy had just married her best friend, and I was truly happy for her. But I was so over love at this point.

My mother stood next to me at the bar along the far wall, watching guests drift toward their tables.

I ordered a margarita from the bartender and Mom ordered a club soda.

"You really should drink less, Lily."

"It was one night. I overdid it one time, Mom." And I'd never do it again, even if the only reason was so I wouldn't have to hear about it again. I admit when Alex broke my heart, I went a little too far with that, but now I was over it.

Once we got our drinks, Mom leaned in and whispered, "Why don't you ask that nice man over there to dance?"

Mom was well-meaning, but she had a bad habit of interfering.

"Your father said he was talking to him earlier, and he works in real estate. That's a good field." Mom paused to sip her soda. "I wish Amy hadn't chosen this shade of red as the wedding color. If that guy over there saw you in your teal dress, he'd march right over here." She glanced around the room. "Red is not a color for a summer wedding anyway. It looks like Valentine's Day in here."

"Amy loves red," I said.

I'd have loved a wedding like this, but it wasn't meant to be.

"It isn't February, it's July." She nudged me in the elbow and lowered her voice. "If we are lucky, we'll soon have a wedding to plan for your sister."

"I'll leave that to you." Mom would love nothing more than to plan a wedding. It hadn't been easy to tell her Alex and I weren't going to get married. I wanted to move on but didn't want to be set up.

Especially not at a wedding.

"Where is your father?" Mom glanced around and then pointed to where he was speaking with his sister, Aunt Lillian. "There he is. I need to speak to her too."

Then she headed in their direction. Aunt Lillian had asked me to perform at this wedding and I couldn't say no to my favorite aunt, or a chance to sing. I was sort of named after her. My name is Lily Anne. It had been my father's idea to compromise with my mother. I'm named after her—but not, at the same time.

I pulled the card with my seat assignment out of my clutch Table 13, Seat 6.

My sister Dana came up beside me and peeked over my shoulder.

"I'm afraid your seating assignment is over at the singles table of shame."

"Ha. Ha."

Dana was trying to be funny. Shameful or not, the singles table was where I wanted to be right now.

She'd told me on the plane from San Diego she would be married well before my age. I was only twenty-eight and she was two years behind me. She was gorgeous—and never single.

I never set a goal to be married at any particular age, but I had expectations after all my time with Alex. But now, I was convinced I was better off on my own.

Dana and her new boyfriend Chad sat with me on the plane ride from San Diego, not taking their eyes or hands off each other. I wasn't sure if Alex and I had ever been like that.

Dana flipped her long hair over her shoulders and leaned in to show me her phone.

"My friend follows this travel blogger online and she sent me this latest post." She pointed to the screen. There was the man I'd devoted so much to, shirtless on a beach, with his arms wrapped around a bleach blonde smiling like she was in a commercial for whitening strips. They looked so happy.

"Is that the girl he was cheating with?" Dana asked.

"That's her." Nice of her to take out my trash.

"She has some great travel tips on her website." Dana scrolled down through more of the woman's posts. "How do people become influencers? I'd be so good at that. I take the best selfies."

Dana was easily distracted.

I sipped on my drink, not caring to see any more of what Alex was up to now.

Alex and I had dated in high school, broken up when we went to different colleges, then reconnected and dated again over the last eighteen months. I'd been expecting an engagement ring from him, but instead, he was suddenly honest with me about being in love with someone else. He'd been dating her on the side for months.

The jackass.

Dana said she was going to find Chad so I went to find my table. I wandered by each table, checking the numbers. Each had a slim, silver sign holder clutching a card that showed the table numbers in gold.

Once I reached number six, there were two empty seats, one for me. A teenager was slouched in the chair to my left, glued to his phone; next to him was a middle-aged woman who was locked into a conversation with a younger lady, probably not older than twenty, on her other side beside her. Only half of her was visible around the large, flowery centerpiece. Another young man was next to her, with earbuds in, oblivious to the rest of us.

I gripped the back of my chair and no one at the table said anything. Only the middle-aged woman glanced up, then returned to her conversation.

"Hey, are you the one who performed at the ceremony?" A man with dark hair in a sleek black suit and tie stepped beside me. He had brown eyes that captivated my attention, like a sea of caramel I could be swept away in.

I nodded and adjusted one of the thin straps of my little red dress. He was probably around my age. He was also holding a drink from the bar and he wasn't wearing a ring.

But why should I care to notice that? Being single was good for me right now.

"You're very talented," he said with a smile that disarmed me. "Are you a professional?"

"I perform at weddings like this occasionally. The bride is my cousin. I'm a high school music teacher."

"That's amazing. I'd love to hear you sing again. Much more than the weird songs this DJ is playing." He gestured to a young man with long blond hair, wearing a bright green bandana over his forehead under his headphones as he worked the sound system. He was playing a rap version of *Endless Love*.

"Is it the rap music, or this song in particular?"

He chuckled. "I've just gone through a bad breakup, so *Endless Love* sounds like a big lie."

"I hear that. My cheating ex is on the beach right now with a woman whose teeth are so white you can probably see them from space."

"Wow. Is it like that episode of *Friends* where Ross's teeth glowed in the dark?"

"Yep."

"I'm sorry." His eyes were so tender. And the room seemed so much warmer.

I took a sip from my margarita. "I'm sorry you're going through a hard time."

"I'm not here for sympathy. I know a wedding isn't the place to avoid sappy love songs. I shouldn't have complained about it."

"No, I get it." It wasn't that long ago I was watching a soap opera and eating an entire box of Klondike bars.

"You seemed like you really love performing."

"No matter what I'm going through I love singing."

"Have you always loved it?"

I nodded. "I've been playing piano since I was in first grade and singing for whoever would listen long before that. Music is in my soul."

He nodded and smiled. "I could tell."

Endless Love finally ended, and a bouncy Latin dance song sounded from the speakers. Dana was already on the dance floor with Chad.

"Are you a friend of the bride or groom?" I asked.

"The groom. Kyle and I met in law school in Albuquerque."

"So you're a lawyer too?"

He nodded. "I'm in contract law. I negotiate, draft, and review contracts. Not nearly as interesting as your work."

Was this a line?

"I hope I'm not being too forward. I'd really like to know more about you." He set down his drink and held out a hand to me. "I'm Joel Velásquez."

"Nice to meet you." I gripped his hand to shake it, and my nerves buzzed. His olive skin was so soft and warm that I nearly forgot my name. "I...I'm Lily Rawlings." My hand retreated to my lap and I cleared my throat. "Do you still live in Albuquerque?"

"I grew up and went to college there, but now I live in Phoenix. What about you?"

"I'm from San Diego, and I'm still there."

"Do you like to dance, Lily?" Joel asked.

"Yes." I was still holding his hand. I probably should have let go sooner. But he didn't seem weirded out. His dreamy eyes were locked with mine. "I *do* like to dance."

"I only know one dance." He paused and I held my breath. "The salsa."

"I haven't tried it before."

"I'd be happy to show you."

My heart was dancing already. Was there a sexier dance beside the Tango? The salsa was sure to be even hotter with a smokin' hot available guy.

What was it that I said to myself earlier about being single and it being good for me? Things were becoming complicated.

He took my hand and showed me a few of his moves, and I followed along the best I could. I was entranced with the way he swung his hips and the light, easy movement of his feet. By the end of the song, sweat was dripping from my forehead in the most unattractive way possible.

We went back to the table for our drinks.

"Where did you learn to dance like that?" I asked, dabbing my forehead with the cloth napkin from my place setting.

"My mother is an excellent dancer, and she taught me when I was young." He chuckled. "She told me it would help me find a prom date."

"Did it?"

He shook his head.

"I was actually terrible at asking girls to prom."

"Really? I'd have gone for any guy who could dance well in high school. So many were only willing to hold up the wall back then, and it hasn't changed much from what I can tell. I chaperone school dances sometimes."

"How is that?"

"It's mostly entertaining. But some of the teen drama is a bit much. I do love my students."

"You must have such great patience. I have a lot of cousins and there are kids of all ages at our family gatherings. I love my family, but I freely admit it can be overwhelming."

He told me a little more about his large Latino family, and I told him more about life directing a high school choir. We traded stories about the bride and groom and tried to guess what their parents were whispering to each other at the head table.

Another lively song started and I perched my chin on my hand with my elbow on the table. "I may need a little more practice with the salsa."

"You're a fast learner," he said, smiling sideways. "But couldn't we all use a little practice?"

His hand was strong and sent tingles up my arm as he led me out to the dance floor again.

We danced to a Mark Anthony song and we did the Salsa again, but he added a long, low dip. I thought I would die, hanging in his arms like that. My heart may have stopped.

When he pulled me up, my knees wobbled like a newborn fawn. He pulled me close to steady me. His eyes were like magic, holding me spellbound.

He continued to hold me close for the next song, Train's romantic ballad, "Marry Me".

With his arm around my waist, my skin sizzled beneath my dress and the rest of the room melted away.

Chapter One

Lily

ONE YEAR LATER

J oel Velásquez walked through the glass doors of the Paradise Shores Resort lobby in skinny jeans and a black T-shirt, pulling a rolling suitcase behind him. He ran a hand through his hair and gave me an instant flashback of how it felt when I'd last slipped my fingers through it. He'd certainly gotten in even better shape since last I saw him.

I wasn't ready for this. I hadn't even said goodbye before I'd left.

He hadn't seen me yet, and I did what any reasonable person would do. I ducked behind a large potted plant with little red flowers.

My shift was going to be starting soon, and the entrance to the piano bar was at the top of the staircase at the back of the lobby.

I'd have to walk out in open view of the elevators on the right wall. I breathed in and out slowly. Maybe it was time to rip off the bandage and face the awkwardness. Or maybe ditching my pumps right here and dashing barefoot across to the stairs was better.

Would he recognize me from behind?

If only he hadn't walked in with the memories of the most reckless decision of my life.

What was he doing here? My palms began to sweat while my heart pounded. While I knew Paradise Beach was a tourist town, Joel had been at a safe distance in Phoenix. But there he was, standing with his perfectly sculpted muscles showing through his shirt. Memories of the night we met last summer nearly knocked me over like one of the waves outside.

The lobby was filled with tropical flowers and plants, but not nearly enough for a concealed path anywhere. I decided if I shifted the plant some to the right, I could crouch behind a sofa and crawl into the bathroom entrance behind it.

I gripped the ceramic pot and tried to sidle it over. It was heavier than I thought, but I managed to move it. I had to go slowly anyway so he'd be less likely to notice a plant moving. But this was painfully slow. A thorn pricked my bare shoulder. *This thing had thorns?* Just as I yelped, my heel slipped. The plant toppled over with me in a loud crash. The pot cracked and soil spilled out.

Of course.

"Are you okay?" Joel rushed over and crouched beside me as I pushed up from the cold tile. He took my arm to help me up, and the sweet eyes I'd never forget went wide.

"Lily?"

"Joel." I struggled to think about anything other than the heat radiating from his touch and the rich scent of his spicy cologne.

I hated how it could still get to me.

"Uh, hi." He dropped his eyes from mine and let go of me.

"Are...are you all right?"

"I'm fine." Well, seriously humiliated, but physically fine.

He reached out to take the handle of his suitcase.

"Hi." I smoothed my little black dress down, brushing off dirt while my cheeks warmed.

Could meeting him again have gone any worse?

"I didn't expect to see you here."

"I moved here last year, after...well, you know." After I left without even saying goodbye.

"Is your family still in San Diego?"

"Yep. They're about an hour's drive away."

"Are sure you're all right?"

"I'm fine." I needed space so I could think. But space wouldn't be enough. I needed someone to slap me in the face for staring too long at his tempting lips.

"How...how've you been?" he asked, rubbing the back of his neck.

"Fine. You?" I was setting a record for how many times I could say that word.

"I'm good." He watched me as he still held the suitcase handle and rubbed his pant leg with his free hand.

I stared down at my feet a moment, then forced myself to meet his eyes. "So are you here for work or vacation?"

"My family is throwing a 'Luau in Paradise'," he said, making air quotes with his fingers. "We're celebrating my grandmother's one-hundredth birthday."

"Really? That's amazing." It would have been amazing for my grandmother to have lived that long. I'd lost her only six months ago.

"Does she still live in Albuquerque?"

"Yes. She recently moved in with my Tía Carmen. Abuela said she always wanted to have a luau in paradise, and her children were worried about her traveling too much at her age."

"I understand."

He shrugged. "So here we are in Paradise Beach."

"Southern California is close enough to paradise." I wished I could come up with something better to say.

"Are you still teaching music?"

"Yes, I'm teaching at Paradise High. I started a show choir and I love it. I still also teach private lessons, because, you know, why not? You know me and music." I was talking too fast and too much, but my nerves wouldn't let me stop. "Over the summer I play at the piano bar upstairs." I gestured to the stairs in the back of the lobby. "It has an amazing view of the beach. My cousin Chris is the assistant manager here." I gulped. "But that's not why I got the job or anything, it's just a fun fact."

"Oh, I know you have the talent, Lily. I'd love to hear you play again."

Really? My cheeks would never return to their normal color at this point.

"I'll be here till ten." Had I invited him to stop by? Had I lost my mind? This wasn't how people dealt with running into their exes. At least I didn't think so. My knees were turning to rubber.

Just stop talking.

"Sounds nice." He bit his lip and shifted on his feet. "I just checked in, so I should probably go get settled."

"Okay." I nodded quickly. "It was nice to see you again."

I hoped it sounded sincere. My knees threatened to give out on me. Being around him only reminded me of the hottest and most humiliating time of my life. Add to that, I'd been too embarrassed to simply walk over and say 'hello' like a normal person, so, instead, I fell into a plant.

"Nice to see you too." He turned to go back to the elevators and I hated how much I enjoyed watching him walk away.

The room seemed warmer. I needed to sit down before I fell again. A year hadn't diminished his effect on me.

Things between me and Joel had never been simple.

Ten o'clock came and my shift ended. I finished up the song I was playing and gathered up my sheet music. Enrique arrived for the evening show. He was also a singer, and his smooth, jazzy voice was a treat to listen to. I nodded to him as I slid off the bench of the shiny black baby grand.

Since I'd ungracefully encountered Joel again, he was stuck in my mind.

I never should have gone to Amy's wedding. My crazy lapse in judgment never would have happened. I was weak, and Joel was a centrifugal force I was caught up in.

The object of my thoughts was seated at a table near the stage, where he'd been for the past hour.

I still couldn't believe I'd invited him.

He'd taken a phone call, and now his face was long and his muscles tight.

Something was wrong. I stepped down to the marble floor and toward him.

"Are you okay?" I took the seat across from him.

He rubbed his forehead. "I have to go up to the hospital, but I don't know what to do."

"What happened?"

"My mom called to tell me they're at the hospital with Abuela. It's her heart and at her age...Mom made sure to tell me Abuela wants to meet my wife before the end."

"Oh, I'm so sorr—you're married?" I didn't see a ring on his hand.

"No." His voice was flat.

This wasn't good. No one was supposed to know what we did.

"She knows about our *marriage*?" My mouth twisted as I spoke the word. The way it happened shouldn't have been legal.

He tilted his head slightly. "Only that we got married, not...the rest."

"You told them you got married. But not *divorced*?" I blinked. We'd had an agreement not to tell anyone anything.

But if he was going to admit to what we'd done, why not tell the rest?

I sat back and breathed out slowly. "Whoa."

He looked at me seriously. "I didn't tell my family. But my grandma is savvier with social media than anyone ever knew."

"It's on social media?" I grabbed my neck. I couldn't have been more creeped out if he'd told me he used to be in the Blue Man Group. "How is that not telling your family?"

"Not anymore. It wasn't up for long. I just mentioned you were my new wife, no specifics. I took it down the next day when we, you know, talked..."

That was when we agreed to keep it a secret until we knew if we were going to stay together.

"...and came to an understanding about how ashamed you were of us."

"Not of us. How we *became* us."

I was supposed to be giving myself time to be single, instead, I really messed up.

"I agree the way it all happened wasn't something I was proud of, but I was never ashamed of being with you."

Yeah. Sure. In the end, he hadn't wanted me around anymore.

He sighed. "But they don't know much more than that. I've avoid-ed visiting them since. My parents were already angry when they found out I got married without them."

"I told my family I was staying with a friend in Phoenix." I leaned forward with my elbows on the table and rubbed my temples. "For a month. No one asked any follow-up questions about it."

"I'm sorry, Lily."

"Don't you think they'd be happy to hear about our divorce?"

He shook his head. "No. My parents and grandmother are deeply Catholic and very traditional. Neither Abuela nor my parents believe in divorce at all. It was already causing controversy that I got married outside the church. They still talk about my cousin's divorce like a plague they all survived."

Joel himself never seemed very religious. He never went to mass while he was living with me. But I knew he hated making mistakes.

And I was one of them.

The rest of his life had been in perfect order before his girlfriend rejected him, and then I popped into his life.

"I don't know how to tell her yet," he continued. "I didn't want to distract her from her big birthday. She's turning *one hundred*. This could very well be her last birthday celebration."

Words to respond to that were not coming other than, "Oh."

I needed more information, but where should I start? Questions were popping like corn in my brain.

"They think you still live with me in Phoenix," he continued. "Also, that you're from Las Vegas and that we wanted to get married there so it could be in the same chapel as your parents."

"Are you serious? Ew. No. My parents can never know I got married in..." I lowered my voice. "Elvis's Burnin' Love Drive-Thru Wedding Chapel. We would all die of shame."

Dana especially would never let that go.

I rubbed my cheeks as I said the words out loud. My face was burning.

"I didn't tell them the name of the place," he asserted. "Or that it was a drive-through."

"Thank you for that." I clasped my hands under my chin.

"I'm sorry, Lily." He pulled a wedding ring from his pocket and slipped it on his left hand. "I still have this and I thought I would tell them you had to work or something."

We'd both had rings, but we didn't wear them.

"But if my grandmother is near the end, what can I say?"

His sad eyes pulled at my heart. "Listen, you need to go see your grandmother."

"I know." He rubbed his forehead. "My parents didn't think they could have children, and my grandmother always called me her miracle grandchild. I don't have a wife, and I lied about it. How do I break her heart when she may be dying?"

His hand was shaking. He was panicking.

"Okay, take a breath." There only seemed to be one good option at this moment between insanity and possible tragedy.

I hadn't been able to be with my grandmother when she passed, and now it seemed within my power to make an old woman happy. "I'll go with you, but you need to work out your issues."

"No, I can't ask you to do that." He stood and raised a hand.

I jumped to my feet and grabbed his wrist. "Stop arguing, we better get to the hospital now. What if this is your last chance to see your grandmother alive? What if this brings her a little joy in her last hours?"

He blinked but didn't fight me as I pulled him toward the exit.

Chapter Two
Joel

The drive to the hospital was awkwardly silent. I couldn't believe I'd run into Lily again.

Despite acknowledging how dumb we were to get married so soon after we'd met, we'd both been too prideful to give up right away and apply for an annulment. The challenge we set for ourselves was thirty days of marriage, to see if we could last. Once we reached that number, we'd fought.

The next day, Lily was gone without saying goodbye.

Once she'd left, it hit me harder than I'd realized it would.

I was an attorney for a large corporation in Phoenix, and I had a reputation for being meticulous and cautious. I was called a perfectionist but I didn't think that was a bad thing. Especially considering what I did with it.

My relationship with Lily had been anything but cautious and rational. How could I admit to anyone I worked with what I'd done one weekend I went to my friend's wedding?

For the thirty days I spent married to Lily, I didn't wear the ring we'd so hastily bought at the only jewelry store open the night of our spontaneous wedding. I didn't want to explain it to anyone. Neither one of us knew if we'd make it.

I also didn't want to end up like my cousin Carlos. I'd sworn to my parents I wouldn't end up like him.

Carlos was the only person I knew of in our family who was divorced. The entire family had loved his wife and they had two adorable kids. Everyone thought they were so happy until they suddenly announced they were not. They split, and his wife moved his two kids to the East coast to be near her parents.

Carlos spiraled into a dark depression and ended up moving into his parents' basement. No one would stop talking about it for months.

My mother would hug me and cry every time she saw me for a couple of weeks. "I cannot imagine the pain of losing two grandchildren. Their mother won't let their abuela speak to them. It's ruining our family."

She then grilled me about how often I was attending mass. This was when I assured my anxious parents that I was far too careful to end up in what I thought was an avoidable situation.

For the next two years, my parents, aunts, and uncles all spoke of Carlos as a cautionary tale. He didn't show up at any family events after he moved into the basement, and his absence only encouraged more of this talk.

I was careful. I had a plan. I dated Kim for a year and a half and planned to marry her. She was a safe, practical choice and we were great for each other. I was convinced, along with my entire family, that we'd spend the rest of our lives together.

Until that time I was down on one knee...and she said no.

Did I cope in a healthy way?

Nope.

I threw caution to the wind in a whirlwind relationship—a marriage to a woman I barely knew—and did what I'd sworn I never would.

It wasn't like me at all.

But there was Lily Rawlings, lighting up the church with her beautiful voice as she sang while her fingers sprinted over the piano keys. I was there to see my friend get married, but Lily in her sparkling red dress absorbed all my attention.

She loved music and threw her whole body into the song for our second dance, grooving like no one else there mattered. Surely everyone was watching. But no one more than me.

Letting out our frustrations with each other, two people who knew nothing about the other's situation, was strangely helpful.

Seeing her enthusiasm for music and life on display was captivating...and sexy beyond reason.

Neither one of us was thinking clearly but caught up in a magnetic attraction. I still don't know why we decided to get married. Did we have too much to drink? Were we in such an irrational state of mind over losing the people we thought were our future?

Whatever the reason, the wedding chapel drive-through was definitely a bad choice.

I had to have been a little drunk when I let the news out on a social media post, however brief.

Part of it was an immature wish to have Kim see me happy without her. I could delete it, but I couldn't take it back. My parents were horrified, of course. I wasn't exactly proud of it myself, but I wouldn't admit it to them. My grandmother simply wanted to know if we were planning to have another wedding at the church. I explained that Lily wasn't Catholic. Mom told me I should fix that.

They were more Catholic than the Pope.

I tapped the brake and slowed the car to a stop at a red light. I had a lot to explain.

"As I said before, I've avoided seeing my family until now." The light turned green and we headed down the road toward the hospital.

"I get it." Lily nodded. "I'm sure you recall that I actively avoid mine."

"I have to tell you something..." This probably wouldn't go well.

"What?"

"I told them you're kind of a workaholic."

"Ha!" she spat out. "You mean *you're* the workaholic."

"I had to say you were working every time my mom called and wanted to talk to you."

"That's all you could think of?"

"What would you rather I'd said?" I really didn't know.

"My preference was for no one to know we ever got married, but if you had to say something, you could have said I was...I don't know...volunteering for something charitable."

"That's pretty similar to working a lot."

"Yeah, but it doesn't make me sound selfish."

"Are you saying I'm selfish?" I asked.

"No, but working all the time when you don't have to, making sure every 'i' is dotted..."

"Okay, I'm sorry I said you were a workaholic."

We reached the hospital and I steered the car into the parking lot. Once I found a space, we hopped out of the car and headed for the entrance.

"I'm an idiot. I kept planning to tell them the truth. I couldn't find the right moment. But there's never going to be a good moment."

"Joel." She patted my tight shoulder, sending a warm spark through my shirt to my skin. "There may be no good time, but it's definitely not the time right now."

We were directed to the second floor where we found my big Latino family scattered about in a waiting area. Adults were talking, teenagers were spread out on the couches looking bored, some of the younger children were coloring at the coffee table in the waiting area, and a few others were wrestling while their parents loudly objected.

My mom stepped forward, her gray-streaked, black hair twisted up in a bun behind her head. She spread out her arms and pulled me into a tight hug. "Mi hijo!"

Mom stepped back to survey Lily up and down. "You must be Lily."

Mom threw her arms around Lily's neck before she could respond. "I'm Eva. I have been dying to meet you. You're so dressed up. You look beautiful. Were you taking her out tonight?" She squinted her eyes and wrinkled her nose at my casual, button-up collar shirt and khaki pants. "Wearing that?"

"I..." I shook my head, my stomach twisting into a tight knot. Lily looked amazing wearing a black cocktail dress with spaghetti straps and matching heels. Nothing about us would give anyone the impression that we belonged together. I couldn't match up with her even in my best suit. She was a knockout.

"He wasn't ready yet." Lily patted me on the chest. "You know how husbands are..."

Mom's sour expression didn't quit. "As I told you on the phone, I will not rest until my only son has a proper church wedding in front of the entire family."

This wasn't the time for this conversation. It never would be. It was my business.

"Mom, how is Abuela?"

"The doctor is seeing her now." Mom's eyes were red and her brow wrinkled in worry. "They're running tests. We'll see what the doctor says when she comes out."

Dad had grown a beard since I'd seen him last. He went to squeeze Mom's hand.

"Joel." He put his arms around me and patted my back, then turned to Lily and offered his hand. "I'm Armando."

Lily shook his hand and smiled. "It's great to meet you."

"Dad, this is Lily."

He nodded. "It's good to finally meet you as well." Then he eyed me sharply. "Your grandmother was deeply disappointed about not being invited to the wedding. We all were. It's high past time you let the family meet your wife, Hijo."

"I understand, Papa, but—"

There's no way any of them would have appreciated that ceremony. They may never know how grateful they should be not to have been invited.

"Hi, I'm Rosa, Joel's cousin." Rosa brushed her long, curly hair behind her shoulders and stepped up beside my father.

"Hello," Lily said.

"I love your dress." Rosa grabbed Lily's left hand and gasped. "Joel didn't buy you a ring?"

"What gives, cuz?" Rosa dropped Lily's hand and placed her hands on her hips.

"Uh..." My mind raced. What could I say?

"I'm a pianist," Lily interjected. "It bothers me to have anything on my fingers that could get in the way."

Was Lily a natural at lying? Or was that true? She seemed so calm.

Rosa raised an eyebrow suspiciously, but before she could say anything else, my father nodded.

"I understand. I have been working on restoring a 1967 Camaro, and I can't stand to wear my ring with gloves on. I can tell you are as serious about your work as I am."

A little pink crept over Lily's cheekbones. "I'm serious about doing what I love."

Other family members stepped forward, and I introduced my mother's older siblings, Carmen, Juanita, Salvador, and Mateo. Then came their spouses and my other cousins and their spouses. My cousins all greeted Lily one by one and introduced their children who were scattered around the room.

"There's zero chance I'll remember all these names," Lily whispered in my ear.

She had to be overwhelmed. She hung on my arm and smiled, greeting everyone pleasantly.

Everyone seemed to be talking at once after that.

"I'm sorry, I know this is a lot," I whispered as I leaned my head against hers. "My mom is the youngest of six children. The oldest, my Tía Marisol passed away last year."

And her son Carlos wasn't the least bit interested in attending family reunions.

"I'm so sorry about your aunt." She turned her face against my ear again. "I can handle it."

My skin zinged from her warm breath, but before I had time to think further, the doctor came out in a bright white coat and adjusted her glasses.

The room went silent.

I couldn't breathe and Lily squeezed my hand, waiting for the news.

"Señora Peralta is going to be fine. She's having heart palpitations. It's uncomfortable, but not serious."

"Praise the Lord," Mom exclaimed as she made the sign of the cross over her face and chest.

Abuela's other children all had questions for the doctor, but once everyone was satisfied that she was going to be okay, the doctor said she could be released immediately.

"We should scale down the luau plans," Carmen said to Juanita. "We don't want to cause her any stress."

"Try telling her to take it slow, I dare you," Juanita said.

"When can we see her?" Mom asked the doctor.

"Right now." The doctor waved a hand toward the door as she stepped back.

Abuela's children went into the room first.

I could only see a little of the room around the crowd, but a head popped into view from the bed, covered in wavy, white hair. "¿Dónde está, Joel?"

I firmly gripped Lily's hand, and the family parted for us to move into the room. My stomach clenched. I'd thought I was coming to say goodbye to Abuela, but I hadn't stopped to consider what would happen if she turned out to be all right.

"Joel! Come introduce me to your beautiful wife." Her wrinkled eyes were tired but bright.

I kissed her on the cheek and she wrapped her arms around my neck, kissing me back. "Abuela, you should lie down."

She sneered. "I've had enough of that. I'm feeling fine. Come, you must be Lily."

"Lily, this is my abuela, Josephina Peralta." I turned to take Lily's hand again and led her closer.

"I'm so happy to meet you, Señora. I'm so sorry about your health."

"Call me Josephina, sweetheart. Come."

Abuela spread out her arms and Lily went closer. Abuela pulled her into a stronger hug than I expected for a woman her age in the hospital.

"Abuela, don't strain yourself."

"Stop fussing over me, Joel. It's taken you long enough to introduce me to your wife."

"I hope you will forgive me for that."

"It's my fault, Josephina." Lily sat on the side of the bed waiting for her to let go. "I work far too much. Outside of my work at the high school, I volunteer at the local community center teaching kids about music."

"I want to hear all about it."

"I direct choir and show choir at...you know, at the high school near us in Phoenix. I also play piano at weddings and other events as well as a piano bar at the hotel..."

"Which hotel?"

"A hotel near our place."

"The Carlisle Inn," I said, trying to help.

"Oh, I can't wait to hear you play. My sweet husband, Gabriel, loved music, and he sang like an angel. I miss him so much. We must find out if the hotel has a piano and you can perform for my birthday."

"They happen to have a piano bar at this resort as well, Abuela."

Lily played with a silver bracelet on her wrist and glanced from me to her feet.

This was going to be complicated, but I smiled through it. This ruse was looking like it would be going on much longer than planned.

Mom came in growling, "Mamá, you must rest."

Abuela shook her head and rambled off loudly in Spanish.

"We can have a small, simple celebration that won't put any more stress on you." Mom folded her arms and groaned.

After arguing some more with my mother in Spanish, Abuela turned to me and said, "I tried an energy drink for the first time this morning, and I suspect it made my heart go wild like that."

Mom went on in Spanish, saying she should have been more careful. Abuela scowled at her daughter. "I only turn one hundred once, Eva. None of us knows how much time we have left. We're going to party like it's 2099."

They began to argue again and I took it as a cue to back out of the room with Lily still holding my arm.

Mom called out to her sisters for backup, and we were able to squeeze out before the room filled with my aunts and uncles.

"You have a lovely family, Joel," Lily whispered to me.

"Really? They aren't freaking you out?"

"Nah," she said with a dismissive wave. "Just be grateful you don't have to meet my parents again."

I'd only briefly met Lily's parents at her cousin's wedding. Beyond a first impression, I knew only what she'd told me about them.

"I wish you were meeting everyone under better, much different circumstances."

Dad came out of the room a few minutes later grumbling and looking exasperated.

I slipped an arm around Lily's shoulders, and as awkward as it felt, it was also familiar.

"We're having a luau after all," Dad shrugged. "Heaven help us all."

Lily excused herself to visit the restroom and Mom pulled me aside.

"Did she ever join the church?"

"No," I admitted. They would either accept Lily the way she was or not at all. "But she's a wonderful woman I don't deserve."

Mama frowned but nodded. "I understand. I trust you are being a good husband?"

"I try." I had tried, hadn't I?

"You know how I *long* for grandchildren."

Oh boy.

"So many years we thought we couldn't have children. Then you came, my little miracle." She pinched my cheek the same way she had since I was a toddler. "I cannot wait to have more little miracles."

She pulled me into a fierce hug, and I felt like scum. How could I tell her I wasn't even still married, not to mention I wouldn't be giving her grandchildren any time soon?

Panic began bubbling up from my stomach. I had so much to figure out.

"It is up to you to be certain they are baptized Catholic."

"Can we talk about this later? We should be focusing on Abuela."

Mom furrowed her brow, but agreed. She pinched my cheek. Did she think I was still five? Being thirty didn't convince her of my maturity level.

I was in so much trouble.

Chapter Three

Lily

I would never have thought that less than a year after I left Joel, I'd be going to meet his ill grandmother at the hospital, leading her to believe I was still his wife. I knew Joel came from a large family, but it was overwhelming to meet them all this way.

Abuela was released from the hospital, and the family members scattered, everyone going to grab something for dinner on their own. I went back to Joel's car, holding onto his arm in an attempt to sell the illusion.

Everything about our real relationship had been a mistake, from the wedding chapel where good taste went to die, to the month of trying to make it work.

He'd taught me how to salsa dance and he was hotter than a habanero on the dance floor. I thought I would get lost in his gorgeous brown eyes. They'd made me forget that worthless guy on the beach with that man-stealing fake blonde.

At one point during the reception, my mom tapped me on the shoulder and recommended I "tone it down".

I admit, making out with Joel in the middle of the dance floor during the bride's dance with her father was out of character for me.

I was usually more worried about what other people thought about me.

Now here I was, Joel's pretend wife, and going off-script again.

Once we were in my car and could talk freely, I didn't know what to say. I was slime. I was lying to his grandmother.

"I'm happy it sounds like your grandma will be okay," I said. "It sounds like we're having a luau together, huh?"

He groaned as he slipped on his seatbelt and leaned his head back in the seat.

"I'm sorry about all this, Lily. I can tell them you had to leave early or that you aren't feeling well."

"But she was so excited about meeting me. I don't think I can disappoint a one-hundred-year-old woman on her birthday. What if she has another episode with her heart?"

"Hopefully it was only the energy drink like she thinks and not something else."

"What can we do?" I reached out and rubbed his shoulder. I jerked my hand back, not wanting to enjoy his touch. "We definitely can't be disappointed she's going to be okay."

"Of course, I'm not, but..."

"I know, it's awkward."

"This is my fault." He shook his head. "I need to be honest with them and fix this."

"You can't tell them now and ruin her birthday. What kind of monster are you? It might be her last one."

"But if not now, when?"

I paused for a moment in thought. How long could we keep this going? "We're only talking about a few days, right?"

"The plan was for a week."

"A whole week for a *birthday party*?"

"It's her one-hundredth birthday luau in paradise, and everyone came from Albuquerque to be here. She's always wanted this."

"Okay, okay. It's only a week, and then sometime after everyone goes home, find a way to tell them we broke up. You don't have to go into the whole story of our past unless you want to. Make it a day she doesn't have any sugar or energy drinks, just in case."

His eyebrows lifted. "Is that your best suggestion?"

"Do you have any better ones?"

"Not really. I've been a terrible Catholic for a long time, but this takes the cake."

"You can go ahead and tell them that too if you want. Get it all out at once."

"I love how easy that sounds." His lips curled in a sideways smile.

My family wasn't very religious, so I could only imagine. My mother and sister were difficult enough without giving them more reasons to be disappointed in me.

A thought came to mind. This ruse may be useful in two ways.

"Well," I said, then cleared my throat. "If we're going to do this, would you care to do me a favor?"

"Name it." His shoulders relaxed. "I more than owe you just for coming up here to the hospital with me. I'd love to help you with something."

"My high school reunion is this week in San Diego. I wasn't planning to go because my ex will be there. But my best friends are going and I'd love to hang out with them."

"You'd like to take a husband to show him you've moved on?"

I hugged myself tightly and wondered how to get this part out. "After we got married I *may* have texted him a photo of us to, you know, show him how I moved on."

"What?" His eyebrows shot up. "You said you didn't tell anyone because they would die of shame."

"I didn't tell him we got married. And as far as I'm concerned, the secret of our Vegas drive-through can die with me. I sent a selfie we took by the "Welcome to Fabulous Las Vegas" sign. It was petty, but I couldn't resist."

"Okay. So am I your boyfriend as far as he's concerned?"

"If you don't mind."

"Well, Lily, if you're willing to make my grandmother happy for her big birthday, I can absolutely help you out with your reunion. Should we make out in the middle of the room as soon as we know he's watching?"

I wouldn't mind kissing him again, but he couldn't know that.

"I'm sure that won't be necessary." I knew my warm cheeks were blushing, and I hated that. But worse than that, I realized how much I wouldn't mind kissing him again.

"Is he the one who cheated on you? Alex?"

"Yeah." I didn't want to talk about Alex. "You in?"

"We have a deal."

"I booked all the rooms together far in advance and they're all on the third floor." Eva pinched Joel's shoulder and grinned brightly. "I have the room right across from yours, Querido."

Joel's parents and a few cousins had gathered in the lobby to discuss their plans. Only half of the conversation was in English. I decided I really should learn some Spanish to keep up this week.

But that was a minor concern compared to the fact his mother was going to be right across the hall from Joel's room, meaning I'd have to sneak in early in the morning and sneak out late at night.

"I'll be right back, I have to speak to the front desk about our plans." As Eva scurried off, Joel's cousin Rosa handed me a piece of paper. "Here's the schedule for the week. Let me know if you have any questions." She tapped the bottom corner. My number is down here. I'll see you all in the morning. Buenos noches." She waved, then turned to walk to the elevators to our left.

"Good night."

I perused the list. There were so many activities listed and they sure sounded fun. Since I'd been working at the resort, I'd seen signs about these things but hadn't had the opportunity to do any of them. My shifts were always in the evenings.

Joel stepped closer to me to have a look at the schedule, and he slipped his arm around my shoulders. "My parents always have a firm schedule."

I couldn't deny enjoying being close to him, now that we were past the awkwardness of meeting again. It may have all been a mistake, but the attraction had been very real. So many memories collided, I couldn't keep track. But he wasn't a memory anymore. He was here, smelling of his spicy cologne, holding me as if I were his wife, and making my heart skip just as he had before.

"Are they seriously going to make us go to a tie-dye class?" Joel whispered.

"You're going to love it, Querido." Eva walked over to take Joel's free hand. "Come upstairs, it's getting late."

He dropped his arm from around my shoulders and took my hand while still holding his mother's. We followed Joel's father and two aunts to the elevator and all packed inside.

It was getting real. We needed to go up to our rooms. And I needed to go to Joel's room.

It wasn't a big deal. Of course, I'd been in Joel's room before. Back when we were married for real instead of pretending.

Why was my heart racing?

This had to be the slowest elevator known to mankind. The air seemed thinner.

Joel squeezed my hand as the doors finally slid open.

"I'm exhausted from today." Eva took her husband's hand and we all walked in a group down the hall.

His aunts found their rooms and then Eva and Armando came to their door, meaning Joel's was the one right across.

"Good night, love birds," Armando said.

"Buenos noches, Querido." Eva kissed Joel on both cheeks, then turned to give me one. "So lovely to meet you, Lily."

"You as well."

His father opened the door for Eva as Joel pulled his key card from his wallet. He slipped it in the slot and turned the handle. His parents were standing in their doorway watching us.

Joel opened the door for me and I smiled, stepping inside as if nothing were weird about this at all. "Good night."

"Good night." His parents waved at us, and we waved back until Joel shut the door.

I released the breath I'd been holding and turned around, surveying his room. His suitcase lay on the one king-size bed in the room.

My heart began its impression of a base drum. I had a flashback of being tangled up with Joel the last time we'd shared a hotel room. I rubbed the back of my neck. Was I sweating?

"You okay?" Joel asked.

"Of course," I said too loudly.

I wasn't really going to be staying in here.

Everything is fine.

Nothing looked disturbed from when the maid service had set it up. There was a desk on the wall across from the foot of the bed and a small couch on the other side of the room, near the sliding doors that led to the balcony. It was dark out now, but when the sun came up it was sure to feature an incredible view of the beach.

"This is such a mess." Joel pinched the bridge of his nose and sighed.

"Nah, this room looks perfect."

He sighed and planted his hands on his hips. "Very funny."

"Sorry."

This had to be hard for him. He always had everything in such perfect order.

Aside from that brief time he'd spent eloping with me.

I'd ruined his perfectly planned life.

A lump formed in my throat.

Everything is still fine...

"Hey, it's okay. How late do you think your parents are up?"

He shrugged and went to sit on the couch. "I wouldn't think long."

I followed and sat beside him and showed him the schedule I still held. "We also have a hula class. And we're going to the aquarium and on a dolphin tour. The luau is on Saturday. This sounds so fun. I've never done hula dancing, but I'm on fire with a hula hoop. At least I was when I was younger. I'm excited."

"You are?"

"I've only lived here since last summer." It wasn't long after I returned from my cousin's (and my) wedding that I took a job at Paradise High. "I haven't done any of this yet."

He took the sheet from me. "Is there time to go to your reunion?"

"Yeah, it's on Friday night, and the schedule only has shopping listed in the morning." I paused. There were worry lines on his forehead. "Your family is great."

"They love you so far."

"I don't enjoy spending time with my family, and I'd love to try all of these things with yours."

I don't think I ever went into that much detail about my family, but he'd met my sister at the wedding. She was talking too loudly about all the problems she saw with the reception.

"Is your sister still as pleasant as when I met her?"

"Yes." I groaned and shifted on the couch. "At Thanksgiving, I only stayed for forty-five minutes before I bailed. My parents know my sister has issues, but they don't think any of it's a big deal. My mom is the other problem."

"I remember. What I saw of Dana wasn't pleasant."

I nodded.

"She does have her good points, but she can suck up all the oxygen talking about herself." I crossed my legs and shifted over to lean my elbow on the back of the couch. "Tell me how wonderful it is to be an only child."

"Did you see how many cousins I have?"

"Not the same thing."

"Well, we all grew up relatively close to each other in Albuquerque. Because I grew up hearing I was a 'miracle' child, a lot of times it felt like something I needed to live up to. To be the perfect son."

"I don't remember you telling me this before."

"It's not something I like to discuss."

"I understand. I knew you hated messing up and I suspect from the cleanliness of this room, that you're as meticulous as ever."

"I haven't had time to unpack." He gestured toward the suitcase.

"I know, but five minutes after I'm in a hotel room, my things are everywhere. I don't even know how."

"It's because you always pack too many bags."

"I do not. I have to have plenty of options on vacation for any occasion that might present itself. It's always the right amount."

"I've never known anyone who had more tote bags."

"I'm willing to admit I have a problem with cute bags." I surveyed the room. "I should probably bring some bags over here. Even if no one comes in your room, they might see only one suitcase when you open the door."

"Yeah, there's not a lot of privacy with my parents across the hall-way."

"After I sneak out, if someone sees me, I'll just say I need something from downstairs."

"I can sleep on the couch if you want to stay over." He gestured to the bed as if it were no big deal.

Me? In the same room with Joel overnight? It was not a good idea.

"Do you…" I thought I might choke. "Want me to stay over?"

"Only if you find it more convenient." He held up his hands. "I'm not asking you to do anything you aren't comfortable with."

"I'm sure I can sneak out." I didn't trust myself. I had to make myself look away from his skinny jeans. "Why is your mom calling you 'querido'? What does that mean?"

"It's a term of endearment. It essentially means 'dear'."

"I need to learn some Spanish."

"You don't have to worry about it. My whole family speaks English, and if they ramble or rant in Spanish, it's likely preferable you don't know what they're saying. My mom has a bit of a salty tongue. She gets it from Abuela."

Lily giggled. "Really? That's got to be entertaining. I'm intrigued to learn more about your family, Joel."

"I never imagined you meeting them this way."

"I'd say it was too bad things didn't work out between us." I fidgeted with my silver bracelet. "We didn't know each other very long. Not long enough."

"I know." He nodded. "Marriages like ours seldom work."

"I'm going to need to tell my cousin Chris, you know, so he doesn't make any weird comments about seeing us together. But he won't say anything, I promise."

"You sure?"

"I trust him completely. He's the assistant manager here. There's no way around it. He'll at least want to know why I'm hanging around here so much more than usual. I'll introduce you after I talk to him."

"Okay..." He looked uncertain. "But other than that, no one finds out, right?"

"Right. We better get to know each other again fast, Joel—if you want to make this look like a real marriage. Oh, and I'm going to need help sneaking out." I couldn't resist. I pinched his cheek just as his mother had. "Querido."

We laughed, but then I realized my hand was still on his cheek and our eyes locked.

For a few heartbeats, I couldn't move. Then I dropped my hand and studied it in my lap.

"Why did you leave?"

When I met his gaze again his expression was solemn.

"What do you mean why?" I stiffened. Didn't he know? "Our agreed-upon trial period was up. It didn't work, Joel. You know marriages like that..."

"Yeah. Yeah, I know. I'm sure it was better that way, but..." His eyes dropped to his hands then back up at me. "I was disappointed you didn't at least tell me."

"I'm sorry I didn't handle things better."

"There are a lot of things I could have done differently. I'm sorry too."

In the quiet that followed, I debated asking him what he was thinking. But he wasn't my husband anymore, and it wasn't my business.

I nudged his arm. "Do you think we should have pet names for each other? You know, like querido?"

"Do you have anything in particular you prefer? Sweetheart? Darling?"

"How about my endless love?" I did my best to keep a straight face, but it didn't last.

He cracked up. "I can't. It only took me all this time to finally get the rap version of that out of my head."

"Okay, then. What about, queen of my heart?" I asked. His eyes seemed to sparkle in the dim light. "Or is that over the top?"

"Maybe we should stick with sweetheart."

"Okay, I suppose that will work." I stood up and smoothed down my dress. "How about you be the lookout while I sneak out of here?"

No one was in the hallway, and all the doors were closed. He stayed in the doorway and watched me walk to the elevator at the end of the corridor.

Part of me wished someone would pop their head out, so I'd have to come back. But it was probably better that I left. The spark was still there when his arm was around me and when we whispered to each other, plotting how to make this charade work. My weakness around him in the past had led to such irrational behavior.

It wouldn't be wise to get too close this week.

Chapter Four

Lily

G etting up early was the thing I hated most about the school year, and I had to be in Joel's room pretty early to avoid being caught.

I grumbled under my breath as I walked through the lobby, rolling my suitcase behind me. I was planning to keep it in Joel's room to try for some more authenticity. Plus, it held my bathing suit and a few other clothing items in case I needed to change while I was there.

Having to get here early was worth it to avoid the temptation that was Joel.

I was nervous, but also strangely excited. I'd get a sexy date to take with me to my reunion and a week of fun activities helping a one-hundred-dred-year-old grandmother have a wonderful time celebrating her life.

Focusing on the positives was necessary to keep my mind off of what could go wrong. I didn't know Joel as well as I would have if we'd spent the last year together, and I needed to learn as much as possible.

I'd deleted his number, but for some reason, he still had mine. He texted me last night a little bit about what he'd been doing this past year. He'd joined a group that went biking on the weekends on various trails, which explained how he kept in such good shape. He was also volunteering at an art museum one weekend each month. He hadn't dated except for one blind date with a woman who seemed more interested in talking about her dogs than anything else.

I decided to send him a little about my current life while I rode the elevator to his floor.

Me: Outside of teaching, my life is pretty uninteresting...I tried Pilates but it didn't go well. I still love red.

Joel: You're far more interesting than you realize. You were in all red when I met you. Your nails always were.

My nails were currently crimson. I was glad to know he remembered, and also that he was awake. Otherwise, I wouldn't feel right about just walking in with the key.

Me: You may or may not be interested to know, I moved on to sometimes letting my nails be pink or to a color to mark a certain holiday. What else do you remember?

Joel: I remember that your birthday is March 1st, you love books, and you

tell people you're allergic to cats, but the truth is, they freak you out.

Me: I'd be fine with you forgetting about that one. Do you remember my favorite animal?

Joel: I feel confident that no one will ask me that.

Me: So no one is going to want us to play a newlywed game?

Joel: LOL. If so, my parents will fail. They once argued about what my mom thought my dad's favorite meal was. But yes, I remember how much you love turtles.

Me: I do. But now I also love swans. I saw Swan Lake, the ballet, and I even tried to learn one of the dances, but I'm not very graceful. I still spontaneously start to sing and dance in various locations—including the grocery store when they're playing the radio.

I stopped, cringing after I hit send. I think I did do some dancing back when we went shopping together. And that was far too long for a text. I should have called. Some of my teenage students only send messages written all in emojis, like new age hieroglyphics. When I had to confiscate phones in the choir room, I was at a loss to understand what they'd typed. I didn't know what all the abbreviations and acronyms meant.

I wasn't sure what to do with learning how much he remembered about me. We were only together for just over thirty days nearly a year ago.

He texted back as soon as the elevator opened.

Joel: Not graceful? Please! I've never danced with a partner who learned the salsa as quickly and easily as you. Music makes you come alive like nothing else. It's impossible to forget. Lily, it wasn't all that long ago.

I didn't know what to say. I stepped out into the quiet hallway, then he pinged again.

Joel: I always wished I could sing as well as you. I, on the other hand, sound like a swan when I sing. That's why you never heard me do it.

Me: No way. You said you didn't like to sing, but didn't mention that. Seriously? That honking goosy sound?

Joel: Exactly.

Me: I really doubt it's that bad, but if that's true, you could make a killing in the circus.

Joel: LOL. I'd have too many questions for the clowns.

Me: Such as?

Joel: Was this your first choice for a career? Is clown college real? If not, how does one go about becoming a professional clown?

Me: You have issues, dude.

Joel: I know it.

Me: I'm taking you to the circus 100%.

Joel responded with a series of emojis with goofy faces.

I certainly had issues too. I was wearing my grandmother's diamond wedding band—the one Dana was still green about my having. Grandma gave it to me before she died. It was yellow gold with five diamonds in a row. I loved it because it reminded me of our grandmother, but also because it was the only thing I had that my sister wanted.

Joel and I both had issues.

I paused outside Joel's door, slipped my phone into my pocket, and fingered the key card. If he was awake and expecting me, he would be fully dressed, wouldn't he?

I sent him a quick text just in case:

Me: Wear LOTS of clothes.

If I walked in there and his shirt was off, I'd lose it. I leaned my ear against the door and heard the sound of a zipper.

Was he just now getting dressed?

Then the door moved away, sending me off balance right into him. His arms wrapped around me and pulled me inside, then he closed the door.

"What were you doing?"

I pushed myself away from his strong chest to stand upright. I had to stop falling around this guy. "I wasn't sure if..."

"If I was wearing *lots* of clothes?" He chuckled and stepped back, gesturing to his shirt that had been pulled over at least two other shirts.

"Very funny."

"I wondered if you'd like it. Look, Lily, as your fake husband who doesn't want to freak you out, I promise I will always have clothes on before you get here in the mornings."

"I appreciate that." I tossed my shoulder bag on the desk, then flashed my ring at him. "My grandmother gave me her ring before she passed, so I thought we could use it."

"Perfect."

I sat down at the desk chair and kicked off my sandals. "Is anyone up yet?"

"Nope, as far as I know, no one is. As they get up, they'll likely all wander downstairs to the café."

"Ah, yes, Chris tells me they have a good breakfast buffet."

"When you're ready to eat, it's my treat, all week."

"I'll take full advantage of that, but right now..." I walked around the bed and snatched a pillow from under the comforter and took it to the couch. "I could use a little more sleep."

"You're welcome to lie down..." he gestured to the bed, then quickly folded his arms. "If, you know...you're comfortable."

Hard pass.

"I'm good here." I laid my head down on the couch.

Let's just pretend he didn't just invite me to lie in his bed.

Everything is fine. Or is it?

"Okay," he said, side stepping toward the sliding doors. "I'll go sit out on the balcony and watch the waves."

—— *ele* ——

Joel shook me awake, and I jumped, needing a moment to recall where I was. I heard someone knocking on the door.

"It's my mom," he whispered loudly.

I nodded and sat up, smoothing down my hair as I swung my legs to the floor. I hurried to take Joel's arm as he opened the door.

Was it too much?

"Good morning, hijo." Eva smiled at the sight of us and threw her arms around me. "I'm so happy you were able to get time off work to come."

She held me so tightly, it was hard to breathe. It was awkward, but I hugged her back.

"I never knew teaching music was so much work." She released me and gave Joel a pinch on the cheek, making him squirm and grab his face.

"Joel says you have so many calls for playing at events that it's hard to keep track." Eva's black hair was pulled back in a clip behind her head. She was shorter than me by a few inches, even though she wore sandals with heels.

If I were only as popular as she thought I was as a musician.

"Let me tell you," Eva folded her arms and eyed me seriously. "I know marriage is difficult, but the key to success is making time for each other."

"I agree, Mrs. Velásquez." Perhaps if I agreed with her, she'd move on to something besides our fake marriage. "I will try to cut back."

"My name is Eva Sanchez Peralta. Sanchez from my father and Peralta from my mother. But call me Eva. I insist," she said with a smile. "Come meet us downstairs. We're going to eat at the buffet before the tie-dye class. I don't know why, but Mamá says she's always wanted to learn how to do it." Her eyes widened. "Can you believe that there is anything left for her to try?"

"Abuela's always been adventurous," Joel explained.

"I haven't tried it either," I said. "Let me get my shoes." After we both put on our shoes, we followed Eva to the elevator.

As we coasted down to the lobby, Eva gave us more marriage advice. Unfortunately, the doors opened on every floor on the way down and let someone new in. Yet Eva kept talking.

"When I was a young wife, I was very nervous about pleasing my new husband. It's so important for a man to feel loved and needed."

Like women don't need that too? I met Joel's eyes and he cringed as he mouthed, "I'm sorry."

Once we reached the bottom, Joel and I stepped out and I stopped him with a hand on his arm. "I just need to go get something out of my car."

Eva lifted a dark eyebrow suspiciously. "What did you leave in the car?"

"Um, girl stuff. You know."

"Oh, that. Don't make Joel uncomfortable with those things. Here, son, come with me to the buffet." She looped her arm through his.

Even though it was a fake excuse, Eva's need to somehow shield her son from my being a human female was bizarre.

"Okay." I took a step back. "I'll catch up with you in a little bit."

Joel squinted and raised an eyebrow in my direction, asking a silent question.

"I'll be right back."

"Go, go." Eva waved me away.

I turned and hurried over to the reception desk in the main lobby. Eva was a little much with her advice and probably stuck living in

1950-something. Moving toward the front desk, I continued with my secret mission.

"Is Chris in yet?" Kelly, one of the new young adults working there for the summer, looked up at me from her phone.

"I'm his cousin."

She struck a thumb in the direction of the office behind her. "He's in the office."

I swung around the desk and pounded on his door. "Chris? It's Lily."

"Hey." Chris opened the door and tilted his head to the side. "What are you doing here this early?"

"It's kind of a long story, but I'll give you the short version if you swear you'll never tell a soul."

"What is this?" He lifted his dark eyebrows. "Middle school? Or are the police going to be coming to ask me questions?"

He looked nice in his black suit and blue tie that matched his eyes. "Don't be silly." I nudged him aside as I came in and closed the door behind me.

"Listen, this is a lot, maybe you should sit down."

"You're scaring me." He smoothed down his jacket as he sat down at his messy desk.

I started by telling him about my break-up last year, my depression at the wedding, how low my self-esteem was after that, and flying with Dana. He nodded politely until I got to the part about my drive-through wedding with Joel.

He blinked and sat up straighter, but all he said was, "Are you serious?"

Other than that, he let me finish and reach the finale.

"So," I said, breathing in deeply. "As you might imagine, neither one of us wants to ruin his grandmother's one-hundredth birthday luau.

This is a dream come true for her. I'm pretending we're still married this week. I wanted you to know since you're likely to see me hanging around with Joel and his family. Please don't say anything stupid."

"You know this is crazy, right?" He leaned his elbows on the desk and watched me carefully.

"I know. But what can I do? I told you, I thought I was only going to pretend for a woman's final moments on this earth."

"I agree it's a difficult situation, but..."

I sighed. "Please just don't say anything. He's going to help me out and be my date to my reunion."

"Well, when do I get to meet him? Everyone will assume we know each other already, right?"

"His mom thinks I'm getting feminine hygiene products out of the car, and that she needs to shield my husband from my true self."

He shook his head. "I don't want to know."

"They're at the buffet."

"All you needed to say was that."

"I needed an excuse to get away for a few minutes to talk to you, so calm down. There are no feminine hygiene products anywhere near you."

"I am calm. I'm just trying to process all this new information. I know you have a spontaneous streak in you, Lily, but this is a bit over the top. I'd never guess you'd marry a guy the same day you met or pretend to be in a relationship."

"I agree." Before this, my "spontaneous streak" was more about taking a day trip with little to no planning.

"But..."

"But what?"

"I trust you to figure this out, and I promise I won't screw it up for you. Just let me meet this guy."

"You'll be nice to him, right?"

"When am I not nice to anyone?" With his elbows still on the desk, he lifted his hands out to the sides. "Come on. I run a hotel."

"You made it clear you never liked Alex."

"Don't you agree with me now?"

"Hell yeah, I do," I grumbled. "But you didn't give him a chance. You were right about Alex, but Joel is different. I don't want you to make premature assumptions."

He stared at me blankly for a moment, likely still processing every shocking thing I'd said. "I understand, Lily, but isn't it a red flag that he's lying to his grandmother? Who does that?"

"A man afraid to break his one-hundred-year-old grandmother's heart, that's who. I told him he'd be a monster if he did that. The woman could have a heart attack for real." I paused, glancing down at my grandmother's ring.

"Is this because you still like him?"

"Nope." I shook my head firmly. "Listen, I wasn't honest with my family about what happened after Amy's wedding either. You're the only one who knows about this."

Chris sighed and rubbed his forehead. "How long are you two planning to be together?"

"Just this week. Then he'll go back to Phoenix. Oh, and I'm going to need some time off. I'll get someone to cover for me. I can't be seen working at the piano bar here while I'm supposed to be on vacation."

"Sure," he said, cracking a smile. "Take some vacation time with your ex-husband. Why not?"

Then he laughed. I tried not to join in, but I couldn't help it.

Once he got himself under control, Chris breathed in slowly and deeply, then met my gaze once again. "Can I ask one thing?"

"Sure." After all I'd told him, what could he ask that was more embarrassing?

"Why did you marry him?"

"I...uh..." I wasn't sure. Did I have any great explanations for my rapid Vegas wedding? "I don't know." I leaned back in my chair and fiddled with the ring on my finger. "All I can say is, between my grief of Alex leaving me, and my rotten self-esteem, Joel seemed like the only person who saw the real me and didn't mind the mess." I swallowed hard and met his eyes again. "At least I thought that was true at first. There isn't any logic in it. I know it was irrational and impulsive. I think we both knew that, but at the time," I said with a shrug, "neither one of us cared. I think we both were desperate for happiness. And there was a fair amount of alcohol involved."

And a sizzling hot man who taught me to dance the Salsa.

"Thanks for telling me, Lily." He sat back in his chair. "Do you feel safe with him?"

"I've never felt safer with anyone else."

My quick response surprised me. It was true.

I appreciated my cousin's concern. Saying it all out loud convinced me I needed to call my therapist. But first I needed to concentrate on being my ex-husband's fake wife.

Ugh. Will my therapist keep me on or just quit?

Chapter Five

Joel

Past the pool area, picnic tables were set up on the white sand just before the boardwalk leading to the beach. The tie-dye class was led by a young man wearing a red, white, and blue tie-dyed shirt, along with a matching headband. His long blond hair was twisted up into a messy man bun, and he had a light-colored mustache and beard. A long necklace made of white shells hung over his chest, and he flashed a peace sign in the air.

"Hey, everyone. Welcome to tie-dye!" He walked over to a folding table covered in white shirts and squeeze bottles filled with assorted colors.

Lily and I were set up at one of the picnic tables nearby with a small bucket of water, two white shirts, and more bottles of dye. She gave me an adorable wink, and her smile had my heart doing gymnastics.

I was in trouble.

I didn't need to fall under her spell again. Despite everything, there was nothing more I wanted at that moment than to spend more time getting to know my ex-wife better.

Abuela was at the table next to us with my mom and Tía Juanita. Mom held up a plain white shirt against Abuela's petite body. "It might be a little bit big," she said.

"It might shrink," Tía Juanita said. Her gray-streaked black hair was twisted up tightly at the back of her head, not a single stray hair blowing in the ocean breeze. She'd say it was bad luck.

Tía Carmen and Rosa were seated across from them, examining their white shirts and chatting rapidly in Spanish, arguing over which colors made Carmen's eyes stand out and which ones made Rosa look washed out.

"My name is Phoenix." The hippie instructor strolled back and forth in front of our tables as he spoke.

Abuela raised her hand. "Oh, my grandson Joel lives in Phoenix."

"Cool." Phoenix nodded then spread his arms out wide. "I'm here to tell you all about how awesomely easy it is to tie-dye. You'll love it." He tugged at his shirt. "You're gonna wanna tie-dye every freaking thing you own."

"Love the enthusiasm on this guy," Lily said, poking my shoulder. "I'm ready."

"First, dunk your shirts into the bucket of water I've got on each of the tables." Phoenix tapped the bucket at our table. "Get it nice and wet, then ring it out. After you have your shirt wet, you wanna choose from one of these examples of how to tie it."

Phoenix went back to the head table and picked up a shirt, twisted it into a circle, then secured it with several rubber bands. "This one makes a swirly design. I call it the 'color wheel'." He set it down, then held up another shirt, twisted it lengthwise, and tied it in several sections. "I like to call this 'the snake'." He placed them down on a card table beside him, then held up the finished shirts one by one. "Check it out. Are you loving the color explosion?"

One was a circular splash of green, yellow, and blue, and the other had lines of orange and blue, separated by white gaps.

Abuela clapped her hands. Her smile was radiant on her sweet, wrinkled face.

"I'm loving this." Lily dunked her shirt in the bucket and then squeezed the water out.

Joel raised his eyebrows at me. "You're digging the explosion?"

"I'm about to blow up this shirt, man." She started twisting her shirt into "the snake".

"Sounds groovy."

"Do you think Phoenix is his real name?" Lily whispered.

"I don't know. We should ask."

"No, we shouldn't." She elbowed me and grabbed some rubber bands. "What are you waiting for, man?"

"Can I just watch?" I couldn't imagine wearing anything I made. I had no artistic abilities. I only passed art class in high school because I made an effort.

"Of course not," she scoffed.

"Okay, but I won't promise anything worth looking at." I wet my T-shirt then wrung it out over the bucket. I copied Lily and tried to put rubber bands in the same places along the length.

"Sweet job, man." Phoenix came over to inspect Lily's snake shirt. He stepped over to stand behind her and placed his hands over hers. "You'll want to slide this a little farther up from the end, so you can have a nice color section."

Phoenix helped her move the rubber band a little, but I found his proximity to her uncomfortable. The way he leaned over her shoulder was a bit much. She was my wife as far as he knew, who did this guy think he was? Besides some mythical bird?

Then he stepped back and tapped my shoulder. "What your wife here is doing is perfect, bruh."

"Bruh?" I fumbled with a rubber band and then dropped it on the sand.

"Here, lemme show ya." Phoenix put his arms around me the same way, guiding his hands and leaning over me. He installed two more rubber bands.

"Uh, I don't need any help." I attempted to shift my body away from him. If I were cringing outwardly as well as in, Phoenix didn't notice. I looked to Lily for help, but she was simply grinning, leaning her arm casually over the picnic table.

Phoenix stepped back again, and my muscles relaxed in relief. "Keep it going like that for the entire length of the shirt, bruh."

"I could use a little help, Phoenix." Abuela waved him over, seeming quite eager to have his help.

"That's what I'm here for." He helped Abuela in the same way, with no regard for any level of personal space.

I leaned over to Lily. "How creepy is this?"

"Your abuela looks very happy," she whispered.

My pulse picked up, feeling her warm breath in my ear.

Abuela was smiling between Phoenix's arms and wagged her eyebrows at us when she saw us looking.

"Ew. No." I looked back at Lily as she patted my back.

"Let the woman have a little fun, bruh." She chuckled.

"What is bruh? Is that the new form of bro?"

"I guess. I've heard some of my students use it."

"So you don't think he's in a cult?"

"A tie-dye cult?" Her eyebrows lifted. "Seriously?"

"You don't think the close contact is weird?"

"Maybe he's a hugger." She shrugged, then returned to focus on her shirt. "You know, some people hug everyone."

"Yeah, I hate that." The man needed to learn boundaries. "Besides, he thinks you're my wife."

"That's the point right?"

She tapped on my ring, and let her finger linger over my hand. I rather enjoyed the zing flowing from my fingertip to my chest.

"Yes, and that's why it's disrespectful to hug my wife in front of me."

"You're jealous?"

"No, just..." I struggled with my next words, opening and closing my mouth a few times. I didn't know what it was that I was feeling, except utter frustration. "I'm disoriented, that's all. Hugging isn't part of my culture."

"Interesting."

I followed her gaze over to Abuela, who was now standing facing Phoenix, giving him a solid hug around the chest.

"This is the most fun I've had in years." Abuela still wasn't letting him go. "Muchas gracias!"

"You sure it's not part of your culture?" Lily slipped her arm around my shoulders and squeezed.

Her perfume smelled like springtime. All rational thought left my mind.

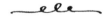

After lunch, Abuela laid down for a nap and my other family members planned to spend the rest of the day on the beach. Lily jumped at the chance.

"I could spend all day every day at the beach if there weren't other things going on in life," she said as we carried our beach supplies over the boardwalk. I'd grabbed a pair of camping chairs and an umbrella at the little beach shop inside the resort. Lily had bought a large, white hat that tied under her chin.

"You would only last so long without a piano," I reminded her.

"True. Making music is really what brings me joy like nothing else. After taking hula, I'd like to learn the ukulele."

"You'd be great at it, I'm sure." Seeing how her heart came alive when she was singing and playing the night we met was the thing that most attracted me to her. I'd sat in the piano bar for the last hour of her shift, enjoying her music until my mom called with the news about Abuela.

"You really should check out the piano bar upstairs. The view during sunset is breathtaking. It feels like playing on the beach, even though I'm above it."

My family members were scattered, and I saw some of my cousins waving at us from the small foamy waves.

"I'm enjoying getting to know your grandmother," Lily said as she unfolded the chairs while I pulled the umbrella out of the long, clear plastic bag.

"She's amazing. But are you sure my big crazy family isn't driving you crazy?"

"No. Are they driving you crazy?"

"I love them, of course, but I wish they had a volume control I could turn down. No one ever stops talking."

Lily laughed.

"I'm relieved this whole thing isn't causing you problems."

"I told my cousin Chris about us. He wants to meet you."

"Oh boy." I thought a moment. "Is that what you were doing when you went to grab something from your car? Or was it really...you know?"

"Yes, I went to see him. There's nothing embarrassing in my car. Come on, you should get over that. I'm a woman. But Chris is cool. You'll like him." She bobbed her head toward the resort behind us. "When we go in, I'll see if he's got some free time."

"I'm a bit worried about what he thinks of me."

"I explained the situation and he gets it." She paused and chewed her lip. "I'm pretty sure."

"You're *pretty sure*?"

"Okay, you have to admit, ours is a hard story to explain."

"Yep."

Rosa trudged over through the white sand in her bare feet. She wore a pink bikini, showing off her brown skin. Her wavy hair was tied up in a ponytail. A camera was strapped around her neck, and she held it up with a large grin.

"I'm taking pictures of everyone. Do you mind giving me a cute couple's pose?"

"Sure." Lily took off her large sunhat and sunglasses, then stood as she smoothed down her long hair. I stood next to her, and Lily wasted no time slipping her arm around my waist and leaning in closer. My pulse was on fire, but I slipped my arm around her and leaned my head against hers.

"Say queso!"

"Queso," we chimed together.

"Perfect," Rosa said, holding up the camera and clicking the shutter button several times. "Beautiful smiles."

I don't think I breathed again until Rosa finished.

"You two are an adorable couple, I just can't stand it." Rosa let the camera hang on her neck and play-punched Joel's free shoulder. "How did you find someone before me, huh? I'm older."

"I'm still surprised." I squeezed Lily's shoulder and kept smiling.

"I have the tickets for the dolphin cruise up in my room. Abuela asked me to pass them out, but I left them upstairs. Just come by my room this evening before you go to bed so you'll have them for Friday."

"Thanks. How much do I owe you?"

"Oh, I didn't buy the tickets. Abuela is paying. I tried to talk her out of spending so much money. She's already paying for the hotel as it is. But she couldn't be talked out of it."

"Sounds like Abuela."

Rosa turned to Lily and lowered her voice. "She sold her house when she moved in with Tía Carmen, and she keeps saying at her age she only wants to have fun."

I didn't like taking Abuela's money, but as I was the youngest of her grandchildren, she'd never let me pay for anything while she was around, despite the fact I had a good job and wanted to help her. She was a magnanimous soul and I loved her dearly. I decided to slip some money to Tía Carmen.

"I'm down the hall at room 435." Rosa chuckled, checking images on her camera. "Oh, Tío Armando gave me some goofy grins. She stepped closer to show us her screen. "So fun, eh?"

"Yes." Lily was still under my arm, fitting as if she were meant to be there. "We'll drop by later."

"Great. I've got more photos to shoot." She turned to go, then swung back. "Don't forget about hula tomorrow morning."

When Rosa walked away, I stepped back from Lily to give her space. The truth was, I needed space. My whole arm was tingling from holding her.

"I've never tried hula before." Lily sank into the beach chair again. "Your abuela is so much fun."

"I was going to say I might be able to get us out of it if you'd like."

"Are you kidding?" She slipped her sunglasses back on. "You have to go, Joel. Think of it as cultural education."

I had to admit, I loved how excited Lily seemed to be about all the activities Abuela planned. Most of the family was here and we had a beautiful beach before us. We didn't need anything else. But this week was about giving Abuela everything she wanted.

"You ready to get in the water?" Lily gripped the arm of her chair closest to me with both hands.

Her smile made my heart flutter. I couldn't say no to her.

I pulled off my T-shirt and Lily lifted her bathing suit cover over her head to reveal a cute mint green bikini. She was gorgeous.

We made our way down to the water, weaving around my cousins' kids. Some of my cousins even had grandkids. Rosa and I were the only single ones. Besides Carlos. The kids were scattered around having fun, some playing in the sand and others splashing in the small waves.

Lily bent over to pick up a seashell, and Tía Juanita, seated in a beach chair a few yards away, jumped to her feet, headed over to us, and snapped, "No, don't. It's bad luck to collect seashells."

"Oh." Lily dropped the shell, letting it fall back to the sand. "I'm sorry if I made you uncomfortable."

"It's not bad luck to collect them," my mom called from behind us. "It's bad luck to decorate your house with them."

"I don't think anyone should collect them either," Tía Juanita said. "I can only imagine what kind of bad luck lies in store for that young man who taught us tie-dye. Did you see his necklace made of shells?"

I stepped closer to Lily and mumbled, "She's rather superstitious."

It was an understatement. My tía was the most superstitious person I knew. I couldn't keep track of everything she thought was bad luck.

"I'm not superstitious, nephew," Tía Juanita huffed. "I am practical. And serious about keeping bad luck and bad spirits away."

"She thinks she's a psychic," Mom said.

Tía Juanita placed her hands on her hips. "Only if being a psychic means I have premonitions from time to time...because I do."

"Oh please." Mom came closer, and she and Tía Juanita continued their conversation.

"You doubt me, but I know full well that Joel and Kim broke up because you gave them that set of knives for Christmas. I told you it would break them up."

"Aye, aye, aye," cried Mom. "Here were go."

I nudged Lily toward the water to get out of the way. "I apologize. I should have warned you about Tía Juanita.

Lily giggled. "I'm sorry for laughing, but they're so funny."

Joel laughed. "I guess."

We kept heading toward the water, farther away from the sisters' argument.

"It's probably good I don't have a sister," I said.

"Sisters are complicated," Lily replied as we slowly waded into the water. "Plenty of ups and downs. My sister is younger, but I feel like I always live in her shadow."

"You won't stay in a shadow, Lily."

"No?"

"When you get on a stage it's clear you're born to shine."

"Ah, shucks," she nudged me. She batted her eyes and I knew she was playing with me.

"I'm serious."

"You like shadows, don't you? Your house was always black and white. I bought all those lamps and it still seemed too dark."

"Perhaps you'd be interested to know, I've upgraded to gray and white."

"Gray?" She scoffed and threw her hands out. "It's essentially diet black."

"It's a valid color."

We kept moving forward, getting up to our knees in the water.

"For boring town," she said.

"I like the contrast of gray and white together. It's a very clean design." I gestured to my gray swim shorts. "See? It works with a lot of things."

"You make such a strong case for dull."

"You gave it a good shot trying to bring in more colors to my place." She laughed. "I did try."

Should I mention I still had those neon green throw pillows she'd bought? I wrestled with whether I should let her read anything into that. I didn't even know what it meant that I kept them.

Once we got up to my waist, she splashed me in the face and said, "The ocean is gray today too. What do you think?"

Her eyes sparkled when she was trying to make me laugh. I loved it. We swam a little but mostly bounced up and down with the waves. A stronger wave hit, and Lily was knocked over right into my chest. We both went under, and the sand slipped out from under my feet. Once I regained my stance, I pulled her up and we both inhaled sharply. I held her for too long, I knew it, but somehow I didn't let go as my whole body warmed in the chilly water.

"You okay?" she asked.

I nodded with my chin on top of her head. "Are you?"

"Yeah."

Then another wave came and we broke apart and coasted with it. I dunked my head down in the water to try to take my mind off the feel of her body against my chest.

Chapter Six

Joel

When we walked back to the hotel from the beach, I was ready for a shower. We'd toweled off so we weren't dripping wet and were headed to the elevator when Lily spotted her cousin at the front desk.

"There's Chris," Lily said, pointing toward the front desk and tugging on my arm.

I was in my sandy T-shirt, swim shorts, and flip-flops, but Lily seemed excited to introduce me, so I followed her to the desk. I tried to comb my beach hair down with my fingers but it was likely a hopeless wreck.

It wasn't yet check-in time, and only a few guests were in the lobby chatting by the elevator.

Chris was alone at the desk and smiled when he saw us. His hair was a little lighter brown than Lily's, and it was cut short. I wished mine was shorter instead of the unruly mess it was atop my head. He wore a white collared shirt with a silky black tie and slacks to match.

"Joel," Lily said, taking my arm and leading me forward. "This is my cousin, Chris Rawlings. Chris, this is Joel Velásquez."

"I'm happy to meet Lily's *husband*." His lips quirked into a sideways smile as he made quotation marks in the air with his fingers.

Lily grabbed his hands and pulled them down. "Geez, man. What if someone sees?" She turned to check around the lobby. It was only us besides an older man at a distance reading a newspaper on one of the sofas. "We're sorry if this puts you in an awkward position."

"I'll be fine," Chris said with a shrug. "As long as Aunt Maureen doesn't show up asking questions."

"My mom doesn't even know I work here." Lily wrinkled her nose at the thought.

"You don't think she'd come by to visit her favorite nephew?"

"Nah." Lily waved the thought away with her hand. "You're confusing yourself with her other nephews."

"Very funny." Chris turned to the side and pulled two tickets out of a drawer. "How about I hook you two up with passes to eat at the French restaurant upstairs?"

"Oh, no, you don't need to give us any special treatment," Joel said.

"Take them," Chris insisted, giving Joel the tickets. "If you want to fool anyone, you should take your fake wife out for dinner."

"I'd be more than happy to pay for a dinner out."

"You can eat right here," Chris said. "Where I can keep an eye on you two."

"I don't need a babysitter, Chris," Lily said. "All you have to do is not ask any dumb questions if you see me holding Joel's hand as we walk through the lobby."

"I'll keep your secret, Lily." He placed both hands on his chest. "But asking dumb questions is my way of life."

Lily groaned and turned to me. "This is my family."

I couldn't help but laugh. I reached out to shake his hand. "I like you, Chris."

"Happy to meet you, Joel." Chris narrowed his eyes and pointed his finger at Joel. "Be good to my cousin. I'm watching you."

"I wouldn't expect any less."

Lily shook her head and folded her arms. "I'll take care of myself, guys."

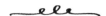

The next morning, Lily was in my room early again—dressed in black leggings and a T-shirt, before any of my family members were up. We ended up watching a morning news show and making fun of the politician they interviewed.

A knock sounded on the door and Rosa called out, "Open up, I hear the TV."

"Please excuse my cousin." I groaned as I went to the door. "Some of us do have manners."

Rosa's eyes were bright when I answered. "Whose ready to hula?" She lifted herself on her toes to see over my shoulder. "Where's Lily?"

"Here!" Lily hopped over to my side.

"Are you as excited as I am?" Rosa asked.

"More, I think." Lily's grin was infectious and I couldn't help smiling. "I love any excuse to dance."

I could dance, yes, but hula?

"We don't have to wear grass skirts, right?"

"I'll find one for you, don't worry," Rosa teased and slapped him on the back.

"I'd love a grass skirt," Lily said.

"You better keep this one, Cuz." Rosa glanced from Lily to me and nudged my shoulder. "Let's get some breakfast before the class starts."

She took Lily by the hand and pulled her out into the hallway. I followed them downstairs and felt like a third wheel. Rosa and Lily seemed to have so much in common. They chatted on the way down to breakfast as well as while we ate.

Lily seemed to be having so much fun with my relatives. Sadness hit me. I wasn't expecting it. Rosa's comment about keeping Lily made me wonder how hard this would be on my whole family once they learned the truth. Sometime after this I'd have to tell them we broke up. Unless I finally told them we broke up last year and weren't really together now. Rosa seemed to be building a relationship with Lily that I hadn't anticipated.

But I should have. Lily was a lot of fun to be around, and Rosa was also a high school teacher.

I barely got a word in as they talked about their students and the various ups and downs of teaching.

"Get ready to hula." Tía Juanita walked by our table and clapped her hands. "¡Vámanos!"

The family was due to gather on the beach this time. As we made our way outside, I took Lily's hand. This was the fun part. I could hold her hand and she wouldn't think it was weird. Or maybe she did. This whole thing was weird. But I loved the way it fit so perfectly in mine.

Mom and Tía Juanita walked on either side of Abuela and held her hands as they led her past the pool area and down the sandy path beside the boardwalk leading to the beach. Abuela protested that she didn't need any help, but her daughters didn't leave her side.

I led Lily up the wooden stairs of the boardwalk so we could see the expansive view of the blue-green ocean at the top. Only a few fluffy white clouds dotted the blue sky. Gray pelicans glided over us in a row, effortlessly riding the wind.

"It's beautiful here," I said.

Lily nodded, still holding my hand. "I'll never be tired of the beach. I would go every day if I could."

"It's been too long since I've been to the ocean."

"Do you still enjoy life in the desert?" she asked.

"I suppose." I met her eyes and shrugged. "I work in an office all day with a view of the building next door." I waved my hand toward the water. "You can't beat this."

"Wait till you try the dancing." She used her chin to point toward my large family, gathering on the sand in a noisy group.

"Why does Abuela want to do this right after she got out of the hospital?"

"The doctor did say she was fine. She wants to have fun and I understand that. She's earned this. But I hope she doesn't take this too far."

"We'll have to watch her. Come on, let's see if they have grass skirts for us."

She pulled on my hand, leading me to the steps on the other side of the boardwalk.

Once we were down on the soft sand, we trudged our way over to the class. My dad was arguing with my mom about why he needed to be here when he could be going fishing. This led to a chain reaction when my tíos joined in on the request to leave.

My mother let loose one of her famous, loud whistles and all were silent. "No one is leaving!" she shouted. "You're going to hula. I don't care if it kills you." Her eyes went wide and she laid a hand over her mouth. "Forgive me for shouting, Mamá," she said to Abuela who wore a solemn expression.

"If they don't want to hula..." Abuela began.

"Armando would *love* to hula," Mom insisted. "Wouldn't you, Armando?"

I wouldn't have refused my mother anything if she were giving me the look she was shooting my father with.

"We all want you to have a wonderful birthday," Dad said, taking Abuela's hands.

"If you'd rather go fishing, it's fine, Armando."

He glanced at my mother and said, "I'd better stay."

"But could I go fishing?" Tío Mateo asked.

"As long as you don't miss dinner." Abuela waved her tiny hand. "Go have fun."

It was then my father and Tío Mateo made a run for it.

My mother scowled, but Abuela wrapped her little arm around Mom. "It's fine. Really."

A young woman with long black hair, wearing a pink flower-patterned sports bra and matching leggings stepped to the front of the class. There were no grass skirts to be seen as far as I could tell.

"Aloha! My name is Nalani and I'll be showing you some hula basics. I have Phoenix here to help me out." She gestured to our hippie tie-dye instructor as he stepped forward and waved to the class.

"For Native Hawaiians," Nalani continued, "hula's origins are deeply spiritual. It tells the creation stories of our islands as well as the history of our ancestors. Phoenix will be helping us with mele. It's poetry spoken during the dance because hula is movement married with the spoken word."

Phoenix was smiling so widely you'd swear his face was stuck.

I leaned over to Lily and whispered, "Is this guy everywhere?"

Phoenix had the beginnings of a beard on his face. His hair was hanging at his shoulders and he sported an orange and white, tie-dyed shirt and skinny jean shorts.

"He is great with tie-dye." She motioned toward him. "I mean, look at his shirt."

"It's nice."

Nalani tapped around on her phone, then a cheerful ukulele tune sounded from a small speaker on the sand. She placed her phone beside it and spread out her hands as she stepped into position.

"Place your feet about four inches apart just as you see me doing. Now bend your knees slightly, and put your hands on your hips."

I looked over my left shoulder and saw my mother and my aunts hovering over Abuela. Abuela was brushing them away. "Stop fussing. I got this."

Abuela copied Nalani's pose, determined to give it a try.

"We'll go slowly." Nalani took a step to the right. "We'll use a four-beat pattern like this: Step to the right, then bring your left foot over to tap your right foot. Next, take another step to the right. Only about eight inches for each step."

"I feel like I need a measuring tape." I felt silly.

Lily poked me. "Just feel the beat. You taught me to salsa, remember?"

"It's the only dance I know." Okay, maybe not entirely true. My Mom signed me up for a tap dancing class when I was a kid. It would be interesting to see how much I remembered if I put on a pair of tap shoes.

"Now go to the left and do the same thing. And try a little swing in your hips." Nalani gazed at Abuela with concern. "Keep it small. Don't overdo anything." Nalani swayed her hips slowly and smoothly as she made her steps to the left. "It helps to keep your knees bent. Don't bend down far at all."

Phoenix fumbled through the words as he read from a notepad. "A Kealia...uh...aku nei au la...ummm...I ka pua ana..." Next, he switched to uttering "ums" and "uhs", but in time to the ukulele beat.

Nalani frowned at him but kept dancing from side to side. "Feel the rhythm of the music flow throughout your entire body."

"I'm feeling it," Lily said. She was doing well—sizzling in her black leggings, swaying her hips in a sensual dance. Lily winked at me, making my heart flip. She was irresistible.

I found myself wishing this was a dance where I could hold her in my arms. I'd danced every dance with her at Amy and Kyle's wedding. We could have burned a trench through the dance floor.

My abuela, mother, tías, and tíos, wobbled around, looking more like ducks marching than people dancing. I could only imagine what I looked like. I was a highly distracted hula student.

A young couple set up a beach umbrella nearby and watched with a smile. Surely the gesture was out of humor from watching how my family butchered a traditional Hawaiian dance, and not out of entertainment.

"You're overdoing it, Mamá," my mother complained.

Abuela rolled her eyes. "You're not moving your hips enough, Eva."

"Now bring up your right hand, elbow straight out to the side like so." Nalani lifted her hand as an example. "Your hand should be facing down in front of the right side of your chest. Extend your other arm, palm down, fingers together." She waited for us to copy her. "Now step to the left."

I put my arm out in the wrong direction and whacked it into Lily's. "Oh, I'm sorry."

"Your left," she said. "Sway those hips more."

I couldn't resist exaggerating the movement of my hips to mess with her.

She smiled and swung her hips deeper.

"Not too much," Nalani said, glancing from me to Abuela. "Only a little sway is needed."

"Keep it moving, Joel," Abuela cheered me on and giggled.

Lily and I were both laughing now, and I kept my eyes on her for so long, the group turned back to the right while I kept stepping the other way.

"To the right!" Nalani called out. "Switch to your opposite hands."

"Oo, ah, um..." Phoenix called out.

"Our helper needs a little more practice with mele." Nalani spoke louder to be heard over him while he mumbled his nonsense. "But focus on swaying to the beat."

Abuela was limited with her hips, but she made wave motions with her arms from side-to-side as she followed the steps.

"Aloha," she sang out.

"Aloha!" Nalani responded with a bright smile. "I'm so happy you're all here with me on this beautiful day."

"Ooo, laa, moo, ahhh," Phoenix continued.

"Okay, that's plenty for today, Phoenix." Nalani interrupted her dance to snatch the notepad from him. "Why don't you help pass out the leis to everyone?"

"Cool." He gave her two thumbs up, then jogged over to the back of the group. A cardboard box overflowed with colorful leis.

Abuela was becoming a little winded, and Nalani called for everyone to take a break. There was a folding chair lying flat on the sand behind her, and she snatched it up, unfolded it, then brought it to Abuela. Mom helped her sit down.

"Why is everyone making a fuss about me?" she complained. Then she smiled over at me. "You should practice your moves some more, Joel. Follow the lead of your lovely wife."

"That's so sweet." Lily beamed.

"You're a natural." Abuela leaned back and sighed. "You remind me of myself when I was younger. I have always loved to dance."

Lily nodded. "I can tell."

"I simply loved watching you dance, Lily," Abuela said.

I thought about how beautiful she was, swaying her hips and moving with the beat in the slow, steady, sensual rhythm. She'd caught me staring at her once, and she widened her eyes, but I only shrugged. I wasn't going to apologize for finding her adorable.

I couldn't agree with Abuela more.

Chapter Seven

Lily

Joel got a text as we were on the way back up to his room that the family was meeting downstairs by the pool for dinner in an hour.

He let me shower and change in the bathroom first. Once I was out, he went in, and I went to work plugging in my hairdryer under the desk, then using the mirror on the wall above it to comb and dry my hair.

When I started on my makeup, my phone chimed over and over. I checked the screen and saw a group text from my sister to me and our parents. She'd sent about ten pictures of herself in different dresses. As I scrolled through them, another one popped up. She followed all the pictures with: **All of these look amazing on me! I can't decide.**

I put the phone down and rubbed my temples. The last time I'd started a family group text about plans for Thanksgiving, I'd included a photo of myself with a turkey at the zoo.

Dana had texted seconds later to say she was too tired to deal with all the notifications on her phone and asked me to start a new group text without her in it. She also said I should do something about the circles under my eyes, and that my haircut made my face look puffy.

I'd made an appointment at the salon right after that and put cucumber slices on my eyes that night.

My phone was now blowing up with my mother telling Dana how gorgeous she was. Dad never answered texts. If you wanted his reaction to something you had to call. He still thought that was the only thing a cell phone should be for.

I didn't want to think about what he'd think of my marriage, divorce, and fake marriage. This pretend relationship was actually going better than our brief real one had. We hadn't fought once this time. Of course, we weren't living together this time either, just briefly sharing a room during the day.

He wasn't dealing with me bringing brightly colored pillows, knickknacks, and throw blankets into his black-and-white world, or disrupting his perfectly planned life.

The thought of seeing Alex again at my upcoming reunion wasn't pleasant, but I knew I wouldn't cry anymore that he wasn't mine. No part of me wanted him back. But I did love the idea of having him see me with an incredibly handsome man who actually respected me.

Joel came out of the bathroom wearing a navy blue shirt and cargo shorts. His damp, jet-black hair glistened in the sunlight pouring into the room from the balcony.

My throat tightened a bit. I had to say something. "Hey, good job branching out to a new color besides gray."

"You mean it's not gray?" He pinched his shirt and chuckled. "There, I'm not as boring as you say."

"I don't think you're boring. I'm teasing you. But, you do realize you'll need something uber colorful and flowery to wear to the luau, right?"

"Ack." His nose wrinkled. "You're right."

"Do you still have your lei from the hula class?"

"Nope. I threw it out. I don't like clutter."

I nodded. Mine was in my bag. I glanced down...oops, it was actually sticking out from under the bed. I met his eyes again, hoping he didn't see it.

"You haven't changed much, Joel."

He sat on the bed, something I was too afraid to do, while I finished up with my favorite scarlet lipstick.

"Do I need anything specific to wear to your reunion?"

"It's semi-formal." I sat in the desk chair and turned it around to face him. "So you can wear a gray tie if you must."

"Well, tell me the color you'll be wearing and I'll see if I can find something to match it."

"You sure?" This could be interesting. "The dress I bought for it is pink."

He didn't cringe, only nodded. "I'll find a pink tie then."

"Pastel pink. It's a little softer than pink pink."

"Pink pink?" he asked with a half smile. "You make so much sense. But trust me, I got this."

"I'll have to go by my apartment to get it. I could grab some games while I'm there if you want something to do in the evenings while we wait for your family to go to bed."

"Sounds good. Whatever you'd like to play."

"Even if I want to play Battle of the Sexes?"

"Um..." he paused.

We'd played that before and I knew how much he hated it.

"Do you have Scrabble?"

"No. But I have a card game called Exploding Kittens."

"Who are you?" he asked with a grin.

"Oh, come on. You know there are way better ways to get rid of cats without explosives."

He snorted. I loved making him laugh.

"My friend Eliza sent it to me as a joke," I explained. "Because of my cat allergy."

"Your fake cat allergy."

I held a finger over my lips and he chuckled.

"She sounds like a fun friend," he said.

"Yes. We've been friends since high school. She'll be at the reunion, so I can introduce you."

"Great. Have you made many friends since you moved to Paradise?"

"I've made a few at work. And I've been taking an art class once a week in the evenings at the community center."

"What kind of art?"

"I'm learning to paint." I gestured to the ocean view outside the sliding glass doors along the back wall. "I did one of the beach."

"I'd love to see."

"I'm afraid it's not very good. But it's a very relaxing exercise."

"You always sell yourself short, Lily. I'm sure it's better than you think."

We soon headed downstairs to dinner by the pools. Once we walked out of the glass doors of the lobby, we first passed the winding lazy river, then walked the concrete walk between the two mid-size pools. The breeze smelled of salt water and sunblock. Families were scattered around the pools with kids splashing and jumping in the water. Some parents were swimming with their kids, and others laid back in lounge chairs along the sides.

Joel grasped my hand. Mine fit so comfortably into his. Something inside me said I could get used to this. Having his hand in mine, walking by the ocean...

But none of this was real. I needed to be careful that this charade wasn't confused as anything more than it was.

Joel's family was grouped around the picnic tables on the sand, separated from the pool area with a small whitewashed fence.

A long card table was set up with a buffet piled with food smelling spicy and delicious. Family members were filling their plates as they shuffled down the table one by one.

"Querido," Eva spread her arms wide and enveloped both of us at one. "Lily."

Joel and I tried to hug her back, each of us with our free arm. He didn't let go of my hand.

"It hasn't been that long, has it, Mom?"

Eva released us and kissed Joel on the cheek. "That's only how happy I am to see you. Come, get something to eat. Tío Mateo found a good Mexican restaurant that caters. Look at this spread."

She nudged us toward the line, and Joel took two paper plates at the end and handed one to me. "I hope you're hungry. My family always has too much food."

"Let's do this." I followed him down the slow-moving line.

There were taco shells and tortillas, aluminum foil pans of rice, beans, shredded chicken, and ground beef. Platters held an assortment of toppings and a large pan filled with red-sauce enchiladas made my mouth water. There was another pan with tamales next to it.

At the end of the table, two chest coolers filled with bottled drinks sat on the sand.

I was getting hungrier by the minute as I filled my plate. At the end of the table, Joel grabbed a water bottle and I took a soda.

"Joel! Come sit by me!" Abuela called out. Joel's uncle Mateo helped her sit down on the bench at the table in the center and sat by her other side.

Joel and I obeyed.

As Joel set his plate down beside Abuela, she shook her head. "No, let Lily sit here. I need to get to know her better."

"Of course, Abuela." Joel slid his plate over and took mine from me and placed it beside his grandmother's.

"How are you enjoying the beach?" she asked as I swung my leg over the bench and sat down.

I tried to imagine that I'd spent the last year in Phoenix and not minutes away from the coast. In reality, I'd only spent a month there. "It reminds me of home. I'm from San Diego and I love the ocean."

"I've been to San Diego once," her soft brown eyes twinkled. "My sweet husband took me to the zoo." She paused, squinting her eyes. "But didn't Joel say you were from Las Vegas?"

"Oh." I froze, remembering Joel had mentioned that. I had to think fast. I glanced at Joel's worried face as it began to lose color. "I meant, uh, my parents are from San Diego and I was born there...but grew up in Las Vegas."

"Ah." Josephina nodded, then took a sip of her drink.

Joel's aunts, Carmen and Juanita, sat across from us. Carmen had curly black hair mixed with gray and large turquoise earrings dangling from her ears. Juanita was shorter and her gray hair was twisted into a tight bun.

"Mamá," Carmen said, "you didn't get the spicy pico de gallo did you?"

"You know I like it hot," Abuela asserted.

"But your stomach," Juanita protested. "I was sure to get mild for you."

Abuela leaned over and whispered in my ear, "I'll never get used to my daughters trying to parent me."

She giggled and Carmen rolled her eyes as she adjusted one of her earrings. "Mama...what can we do with you?"

"You can bring me more chips." She lifted her plate and handed it to Carmen. "And more guacamole, if you please."

Carmen pressed her lips together in a tight line but carried the plate back over to the buffet table.

"Tell me about your family, Lily."

I glanced at Joel and I could see the worry in his eyes. His hand was resting on his right leg, and I slipped my fingers through his and gave him a gentle squeeze.

"My dad is an architect in San Diego and my mom works at an art gallery."

I hoped she wouldn't ask if we were close. The answer was complicated. We didn't talk often, and holiday visits were short because I couldn't be around my sister or mother too long without wanting to crawl out the bathroom window.

"Any siblings?"

"I have a younger sister."

I said sister, but I wanted to say demon.

Joel tightened his grip on my hand, his tender eyes meeting mine. His understanding meant a lot.

"Such a small family," Carmen said.

"And what does your sister do?" Abuela took a slow sip from her water bottle.

"She's a photographer." Sort of. She takes zillions of pictures of herself and whatever she's wearing. I didn't want to say she was twenty-six and living with my parents, or that she couldn't hold a job because she thought she was always right.

Carmen returned with the chips and guacamole.

"Now you shouldn't eat too much, Mamá," Juanita said. "It's bad luck."

"You eat too little, Juanita," Abuela said, loading a chip with a good helping of guacamole. "I only got to this age by enjoying life."

"No one knows more about having fun than my abuela," Joel said proudly.

"A little spice is sure to keep the devil away," Abuela said with a bright, wrinkly smile. "Lily, I hope you will help my grandson loosen up a bit. He works so hard, like his father. That's a good thing, yes. But he works too much. But I am hoping, Joel, that you can take more time off to have fun with your wife."

"I'm on vacation, Abuela," Joel said. "I'm taking a break."

"I'm happy you are. And I'm glad to see how happy you are with your beautiful bride."

"Do not let this one scare you off, Lily." She tapped me on the shoulder and smiled, deepening the lines around her eyes. She was adorable.

"Abuela!" Joel whined.

"I love you, my sweet grandson." Abuela reached over to pat his hand. "But you know what I'm talking about."

His jaw was tight as he looked away from Abuela.

Taking pity on him, I came up with some quick lies. "He's been working better hours lately. We've taken several weekend trips and he comes to see my show choir perform."

"Does he? How nice. What is show choir?"

"The students sing and do some light dancing in flashy costumes. Usually with a Broadway tune." I couldn't get enough of Broadway if I tried. I always danced and sang with the students in our practices. "We compete around the state with other choirs and have a lot of fun."

"Oh, I'd love to see. I will have to visit Phoenix."

Joel shifted uneasily between his feet. I didn't know what to say.

I wish I could dig into the sand beneath our feet to hide like a crab. What kind of creep lies to an old woman? Sure, I could invite her to see a show choir performance. But it was at the high school fifteen minutes away from here and not in Phoenix. My parents had never once shown an interest in seeing my students perform, and I loved Abuela's interest. She was so loving and kind, much like my late grandmother. This charade was only lasting for this week, and I didn't know how long Joel would wait to break the news.

"My daughter Carmella loves to sing," Juanita said to me. "She couldn't make it because she moved to Brazil with her new husband. Alas, she took my advice over New Year's and ran around the block with a suitcase."

I was about to ask a question, but she must have seen it in my face because she continued.

"It was supposed to ensure you have many travels in the coming year, of course," she gestured over to me as if I somehow knew this. "But it wasn't supposed to mean she'd fall in love with a musician and move to Brazil. Perhaps she used the wrong kind of luggage?"

"Now, Tía Juanita." Joel dipped his chin and jerked his eyes in my direction. "There's nothing wrong with falling for a musician."

"No, of course not." Juanita reached out and grabbed my hand as I was reaching for my drink. "I have nothing but admiration for you as a musician. Teachers are incredible. My oldest son teaches Spanish. My son-in-law, however, only *thinks* he's a professional musician. But the truth is, he and my only daughter…" she closed her eyes and shook her head, "are living in his parents' basement with a *ridiculously* expensive drum set."

"Living in the basement like Carlos," Carmen whispered with a hand over her mouth.

Juanita shushed her with a stern look. "We don't talk about that."

Carmen sighed and met my eyes. "Well, I'm so glad to see you are so different from Joel's girlfriend Kim."

Joel gulped his soda the wrong way and started coughing.

"She was a sweet girl, don't get me wrong." Carmen's lips twisted. "But she could be...a lot."

That was how Joel described his family. And also something you could say about mine. I wasn't even Joel's wife anymore, but I didn't like Kim being brought up like this. She'd been a sore spot while we were together.

I patted Joel's back while he gained control of his cough. His cheeks were flushed. "Could we not talk about my ex?"

"If only your mother hadn't given you knives for Christmas," Juanita said. "It's bad luck as a gift."

Carmen leaned her head back and glanced at the sky, jingling her earrings then glared at Juanita. "Knives do not mean anyone will break up. It's silly."

"No, Carmen," Juanita warned her sister. "It is bad luck to deny it."

Joel leaned one elbow on the table and rubbed his forehead. I pressed my lips together as tightly as I could.

Do. Not. Laugh.

"Well, if it was the knives, it all worked out for the best," Abuela asserted. "Lily here clearly makes Joel happier than he ever was with Kim."

Joel sat straight up and flushed again, so I rubbed his shoulder.

"They are perfect together." Carmen winked at me.

Joel lifted his fork and focused on pushing it around his plate to avoid my eyes. I wish I knew what he was thinking. Despite how uncomfortable this was, I couldn't deny how good it felt to be wanted. His family seemed to approve of me.

Well, they would for this week. Was it wrong to enjoy something that would end so soon?

Chapter Eight

Joel

The Paradise Aquarium was only a few miles from the resort along the coastal highway. The wide exterior was pastel blue and decorated with colorful fish with cartoon googly eyes. My family caravanned in multiple cars this morning and gathered outside the entrance as Abuela insisted on paying until Tío Mateo talked her down.

"We all have jobs, Mamá," he insisted. "You don't need to take care of us."

Abuela relented and let each family pay for themselves, but she protested when Mom rented a wheelchair for her.

"What do I need that for?" Abuela frowned at it as a young man wearing a collared shirt and an employee badge rolled a chair over to her.

"It is a lot of walking, Mamá," Mom said, spreading out her hands in exasperation. "I'll push you when you are tired."

"You'll get tired before I will."

"Why do you need to be so stubborn?" Mom took the wheelchair from the young man and he rushed back to the office, away from the controversy.

"Why is everyone fussing over me?" Abuela slowly shook her head.

"Come on, Mamá," Tía Carmen wrapped her arm around Abuela. "Just let Eva push you a little."

The argument continued until Abuela huffed and agreed to "rest for a few minutes" if "everyone would shut it".

Then she proceeded to curse in Spanish, and I was glad Lily didn't understand. Shouldn't she have wanted to run away from us by now? Yet there she was beside me, amused and smiling at the scene.

Once I paid for our tickets, I took her hand in mine, enjoying the feeling and hoping I wouldn't miss it.

Last night in my room we'd played her Exploding Kittens game, and I laughed more than I think I ever have in my life. She was funny and witty, and I didn't want to stop talking to her. But once it was two in the morning, she decided it was time to sneak out.

There was too much at stake if I let myself fall for her again. I remembered too well how it all ended. She left without an explanation, but I knew it was because she couldn't stand living with me anymore.

Could we be friends now?

Things seemed to be going well so far. If only my pulse would cooperate instead of increasing when she was leaning against my shoulder and looping her fingers through mine as if we were a real couple.

Most friends didn't have problems like this.

Once past the ticket counter, the path inside led to a long, wide hallway of large fish tanks.

"Are any fish particularly bad luck?" Lily gave me a nudge as we stopped in front of a wall of colorful tropical fish. "Or only if we decorate the house with them?"

"Are we talking art or the real fish?"

Lily wrinkled her nose. "What about both? You could fill your house with aquariums and have paintings of them on all the walls."

"Sounds like bad luck if you're an interior decorator." I didn't know what Tía Juanita would say, but nearly everything seemed to be bad luck with her. "I'm not superstitious. Are you?"

"Nope." She shook her head and then gazed around to make sure the other family members had scattered away from us. "I have seashells in my house, but I won't tell anyone else."

"Good call."

She met my eyes again. "Juanita is so interesting. She seems so serious, and I try not to laugh."

"She's serious, all right. But I don't think anyone else buys into it." I hesitated. "But with my family, who knows?"

"If there's anything I know for sure about you," Lily said, poking my upper arm, "it's how practical you are."

"That's me." I pointed toward a red fish that swam by. "I'm still picturing that house decorated with fish."

"Yeah, have you seen how some people put fish tanks inside the walls? Like this in their house." She pointed to a smaller tank on the wall filled with tiny seahorses.

"It's a nice space saver, for sure."

"I love ocean-themed art. I can picture having it everywhere. The room could be so colorful if there were scenes of tropical fish and coral."

I steered her toward the next tank, another small one embedded in the wall filled with two lobsters ambling around.

"My apartment has no ocean theme whatsoever," she said. "But I've tried to make it colorful. I have a couple of throw pillows shaped like treble clefs that make me quite happy."

I remembered the rainbow of pillows she'd bought for my apartment during our month together. They'd gone with her, and when she was gone, my place was back to gray and white. Everything was clean, but for the first time, nothing about it made me happy.

We came to the next tank filled with blue and yellow fish.

"You know, fish might be my favorite animal," I said.

"Really?"

"They seem like they're probably the cleanest pet to have."

"Hmm." She glanced from me to the lobsters. "You haven't cleaned out an aquarium, have you?"

"Is it that bad?"

She turned back to me with a grin. "Why don't you try taking care of a nice little succulent? It won't make a mess and it doesn't need a lot of water."

"You have no confidence in me having a fish, huh?"

"There isn't an animal that doesn't make a mess. But of all the animals, go with a fish."

There were a few fingerprints on the glass, and it bothered me. I began to ponder how much glass cleaner this place must require.

"Hey, there's your mom." Lily jolted me out of my thoughts.

Mom, Tía Carmen, and Tía Juanita rested on a bench in front of a tank of Jellyfish.

"I wanted to make the cake myself," Tía Carmen said, sliding her curly hair behind her ears, "but it isn't practical to bake in a hotel."

"We don't want a repeat of your competitive cupcake decorating contest," Mom warned.

"Ah, Eva, no spoilers!" Tía Carmen chuckled as we came closer.

"My aunts don't bake much," I told Lily. "But we take our life in our hands if we get in the way of their version of Cupcake Wars."

"Oh, it was never that bad." Tía Juanita dismissed the thought with a flick of her hand.

"That would have been fun to see," said Lily.

"I ordered a nice cake from a bakery in town," Mom said loudly. "No more talk of cupcakes."

"Where is Abuela?" I didn't see her anywhere.

"She is letting your father push her over to see the sharks." Mom rolled her eyes. "After all the protesting, she got right in when he said he'd happily be her chauffeur. But at least she's sitting down and letting someone push her."

"Oh, Lily," Tía Carmen said, getting to her feet. "Mamá would love for you to sing a song at her luau."

"Really?" Lily asked, her voice rising a pitch. "Is she sure?"

"She will insist if you refuse."

"I am honored she's thinking of me for such a special occasion. Is there a song she has in mind?"

"Sing anything you'd like. It will be lovely, I'm sure." Tía Carmen turned back to Mom and Juanita and motioned for them to come. "Well, come on, let's go find these sharks."

The three ladies started down the corridor and we followed at a distance while they discussed their various feelings about sharks.

Lily moved closer to me and whispered. "Does she have a favorite song?"

"I'll find out. Perhaps she has something in mind. I'll talk to her."

"Yes, please do."

"Tía Carmen is right though, anything you sing will make her so happy."

"I don't know about that." Her eyes held a mischievous glint. "Sometimes I sing songs in the shower that should never be sung at anyone's grandmother's birthday celebration."

"Stay away from those, and you'll be fine." I stopped walking and turned to face her. "But if you're not comfortable singing in front of my family, just say the word and I'll get you out of it."

"No, I'll be happy to." She took my hand and led me back on a stroll. "It's a surprise. And it's her one-hundredth birthday. I don't want to mess this up."

"I believe in you, Lily. You'll never do that."

A camera flashed behind us. As we turned to look over our shoulders, we saw Rosa holding her camera to her eye, flashing several more shots.

"Wasn't there a sign about no flash photography?" I blinked several times, willing the dark spots to leave my vision.

"I won't shoot any of the animals with the flash." Rosa clicked a few buttons on her camera and then let it hang from the strap around her neck. "It's off."

She caught up to us, and we paused in front of another aquarium filled with shiny round silver fish grouped in a circular pattern.

"You two make the cutest pictures." She clicked around on her camera and brought up a screen with one of her photos and leaned in between us. "See this one?"

It was an image of Lily and me from behind, holding hands and smiling. We looked so perfect together.

If Rosa only knew.

"Have you always loved photography?" Lily asked her.

"Just in the last few years. I want to start my own business some day and shoot weddings and events."

"You'd be amazing at weddings," Lily said.

"Oh, Joel, you should move back to Albuquerque. What if Lily and I could get booked at the same wedding, her to perform and me to shoot?"

I tried to smile, but it probably wasn't convincing. I didn't want to talk about the future with Lily. There would be no more of us as a couple once our deal was up. Perhaps we'd stay friends, but who knew?

"Someone might misunderstand what you said and think you're talking about a shotgun wedding," Lily said with a little grin.

"Ha!" Rosa slapped her on the shoulder and cackled. After a moment, she focused on me. "Hey, I forgot to ask how you met. It was at your friend's wedding, right?"

That was an easy question.

"Yes, my friend Kyle married Lily's cousin Amy, and we were seated at the same table."

"There must be more to the story than that." She turned to Lily and nudged her. "What's the scoop? What did you think of this guy?"

Lily studied my face, and my muscles tensed as I wondered what she would say.

"Well, as Joel says," Lily began, facing back to Rosa, "we were seated at the same table. My seat was right next to his in fact, and he was...very charming."

"Yes...and?"

Lily closed her eyes and sighed softly. "And, I don't believe in love at first sight, but when I saw Joel..." She opened her eyes again and took Rosa's hand. "I swear the earth moved. It was as if birds were singing his name, and when he asked me to dance..." Her hand moved to the center of her chest and she sighed again, this time making it a little longer. Then she dropped her hand, glanced from me to Rosa, and said, "He asked me to dance and taught me how to Salsa. What woman wouldn't love a man like that?"

I doubted Rosa would buy this. But she proved me wrong.

"It was fate." Rosa was *beaming*. If she smiled any wider her face would crack. "I just know it. Oh, Joel." Rosa slipped her arm around my back and gave me a sideways hug, squeezing me hard. "Don't screw this up."

"I'm doing my best."

Someone in the group farther ahead of us called for Rosa to take more pictures up ahead, so she said a quick goodbye to us and hurried on.

I turned to Lily, who was holding her lips together trying not to laugh.

"Perhaps you should look into teaching drama if you ever get tired of music," I said to her as we kept walking.

"Did I go overboard?"

"Birds were singing my name? Really?" I pulled my phone from my pocket and opened the app I used to make notes and began typing what she'd said.

"What are you typing?"

"I'm making notes about what we've told people."

"You think you'll forget the story of how we met?"

I let out a short laugh. "That's a story I'll never forget, trust me. I just made a note about the bird metaphor."

"I love metaphors. Birds aren't unlucky according to Juanita I hope."

"As far as I know, owls are the only ones she claims are bad omens."

"Good to know. I have a beach towel with little pink owls on it, but I'll be sure not to bring it down to the beach."

"I don't know how she feels about artistic depictions of owls."

"Maybe that's even worse," said Lily smiling.

If birds would ever sing someone's name it would be Lily's when she smiled.

"When I was growing up, my mother's brothers and sisters lived near us, and Tía Juanita always told us to wear red underwear on New Year's Eve for good luck."

"That sounds amazing to have so many aunts and uncles nearby." Lily took my hand and we resumed walking down the hall. "So Juanita believes you broke up with your ex because someone gave you knives?"

"I suppose she does. I never heard her mention it before this trip. She had complained when one of my cousins registered for a knife set for her wedding, but I never thought much about it." I chewed on my lip for a moment, thoughts swirling in my mind.

What had gone wrong with my relationship with Kim had been a source of much soul-searching after she rejected me. Then, after Lily, I was alone again to analyze why I was so bad at relationships. I didn't come up with any great answers besides knowing I'm difficult to live with.

"I remember you told me she was an attorney as well."

"Yes. I thought we made sense and were in love for a while, but by the time I proposed, she didn't feel the same way anymore." We paused in our walk and I turned to face her. "I still feel like an idiot for not seeing it sooner."

"I feel the same way about Alex. I only *thought* he was going to propose. If he had, I probably would have said yes." She lowered her eyes, studying her feet. "If Kim had said yes, and if Alex hadn't cheated on me, we wouldn't have ended up at the singles table."

"You're probably right."

She slowly met my eyes. "But would we have been happy with Kim and Alex?"

"I never realized how incredibly boring Kim really was until I met you, Lily." The truth came out of me without warning.

She slanted her head to one side and narrowed her eyes. "Are you sure about that?"

"Absolutely. Kim couldn't dance to save her life. She never would have even *tried* to hula, and my grandmother didn't like her."

"Oh, if Abuela didn't like her..."

"That should have been my first sign right there. Abuela likes everyone she meets, but she especially likes you."

"Despite all the complicated mess, I'm glad I met you, Joel."

Lily breathed deeply and took both of my elbows in her hands. My nerve endings stirred in my arms. She smelled like sweet coconut and honey.

All I could think about was wanting to pull her in even closer. Her eyes were locked on mine and I slowly inched closer.

Kids began shouting from a hall that branched to our right. "Shark! Shark!"

She dropped her hands and I stepped back. I had trouble meeting her eyes while she bit down on her bottom lip. I'd been so close to kissing her. I hadn't been thinking.

Lily hugged herself and said in a higher voice than usual, "Let's go see."

She headed in the direction of the noise and I followed.

Chapter Nine

Lily

My head was still buzzing from the way he'd looked at me when I nearly hugged him in the aquarium. I hadn't meant for it to be such an intimate moment, but his eyes were so soft and loving, and I thought I saw a hint of hunger.

After we finished touring the aquarium, it was back to the beach where I joined in with Joel, helping some of the younger kids build a sand castle. His youngest little cousin, Bella, kept insisting Joel make the moat deeper, and he tried his best to please her with his digging skills until the plastic shovel snapped. Then he used his hands to carve out a moat until it was to her liking. The bucket-shaped castle had four good towers until Bella's older brother accidentally fell into it while trying to catch a frisbee. Bella cried, and Joel hugged her so sweetly I thought my heart would explode. We both promised her we'd build a bigger, better one. Half way through our build, the kids had run off to play in the water.

Once we finished, we had eight pretty good towers, a nice looking wall to surround it, and a very awesome moat. I declared us expert sand castle builders and said we deserved a swim too. He raced me to it.

On the way back inside, I ducked into the gift shop and found a puzzle I thought Joel would like, then I passed the coffee shop and bought a few slices of cake to take upstairs.

Doors to several cousins' rooms were propped open and kids were running back and forth. Some were rolling toy trucks up and down the hall. Some of Joel's cousins were so much older and had grandkids now so there were plenty of children. I couldn't keep track of who was who.

Joel was joining in on rolling one of the toy trucks and I stopped to watch for a moment. Once the truck crashed and another boy took it, he stood and walked over to me. I showed him the puzzle. It was a thousand-piece painting of a pier stretching out into the ocean at sunset.

He smiled and said, "I love it."

"This one doesn't appear to have any seashells in it."

Joel chuckled. He held tightly to my hand as we weaved around the chaos and waved to the few adults who were peeking their heads out into the hall. We ducked inside his room and closed the door.

It was dark outside, but I pulled open the sliding door to the balcony and left it open to smell the ocean air.

"The air is nice tonight." I inhaled the salty sweetness, then turned to see Joel straightening up the room. I cringed. Somehow my things were all over the place. It was one of the reasons he found me hard to live with before.

"Oh, I'll move my stuff."

"No need, I..." he paused while folding my dry beach towel. "I got it."

I nodded. I'd come in and out of the room when I changed out of my bathing suit in a hurry and hadn't been thinking about what Joel would think about my things tossed around. Even when I wasn't in a hurry, I wasn't known as a neat person. I did try.

I cleared my makeup off the desk and put it back in my suitcase, then carried my bags from the shops to the table.

"I also brought cake." I slid the two clear plastic boxes holding slices of cake out of one bag. "I wasn't sure if you wanted to continue our old habit of rating bakery cakes?"

He grinned. "Yeah, we never really decided which store had the best one."

We used to go shopping together and always grabbed slices of cake from each store's bakery.

"Well," I said, "if you're interested in starting a new contest, this is a carrot cake from the coffee shop downstairs."

"I'm game."

We decided it would be best to eat cake first, then open the puzzle.

"The cream cheese is well proportioned, I say," Joel said, licking his fork.

Oye. This man could distract me.

"What do you think?" he asked.

"I agree. The perfect amount. Should we give them a rating from one to ten? Our old system was kind of dull."

"You mean you didn't like thumbs up or thumbs down?"

"Too simplistic."

He nodded. "I'll give this an eight."

"Eight and a half."

I threw away the cake boxes and opened the puzzle. Then we spread the pieces out on the table. It was close to the sliding door where I could drink in more of the delicious air. "I love the sounds and smells of the ocean."

Joel nodded. "It is such a relaxing sound. I should sleep with the door open like this."

"I'd like to try to paint a scene like this." I began sorting the pieces that went along the edges to one side. "It's so serene."

"I don't think I've tried painting since elementary school."

"It's fun. Though, you may be bored."

"I'd be willing to give it a try," I said.

"Tomorrow night is the reunion, isn't it?"

I nodded, hoping he wasn't going to try to back out.

"Do you want to go over what our story is?" He was sliding brown pieces of the pier into a separate pile.

"How about, after you broke up with your girlfriend, you took a sailboat around the world but you still hadn't found the one. You were singing that U2 song the entire time," I then sang the line wrong on purpose, "I still haven't found the woman for me…" I dragged out the last word for emphasis.

Joel set his elbow on the table and leaned his cheek against his hand and laughed. There was nothing more melodious to me at that moment.

She continued, "You landed on this island, and you ask the advice of a wise elder, and he said the one you are looking for isn't here, but the answer is in California."

"That's all he says?" One of his eyebrows curled up.

I nod, trying to be serious. "That's all."

"Once you sail to California, you happen to land in San Diego."

"Happen?" He lifted one eyebrow. "Didn't my ship have a navigation system?"

"No," I said confidently. "You were following your heart and it led you there."

"Oh, heart navigation. I hear good things."

"That's how it works. It's incredibly useful. In San Diego," I continued, "you find a bottle on the beach with a message inside.

"Do tell."

"The message consists of lyrics from Nelly Furtado's song about being like a bird. You take that as a sign and head to the aviary at the San Diego Zoo."

Joel's face looked like I asked him to solve a Rubix cube while standing on his head. I was losing him.

"And there," I tapped on the table, "inside one of the aviaries, surrounded by tropical plants and flowers, birds in colors you never knew existed fly all around you. You then see me trying to sing with the birds and failing miserably."

He jabbed a finger in my direction. "And there's the most unbelievable part of this story."

"Our eyes meet, the universe speaks, birds chirp in enthusiastic harmony, and we just knew."

Joel laughed again and I loved it. I was giddy.

"But seriously, we'll keep our story that we met at a wedding, but we dated instead of...you know, what we actually did."

"Do you wish we'd dated instead?" His eyes captured mine. I wanted to look away but I couldn't. My eyes drifted to study his lips, recalling how soft they were.

"I do wonder if things would have ended differently if we had." My heart pounded in my throat. I couldn't believe I'd said that out loud. I couldn't read his face as he held my gaze.

"Perhaps," he said. "But we both had healing to do. Back then, we were basing our relationship on the attraction and initial connection we felt. We were both lonely and vulnerable."

"I know you mentioned your family is against divorce, and you didn't want to give up and end our relationship that way. But how do you feel about it now?"

"I think it's a sad reality. It's necessary sometimes. In our case, I suppose it made sense. And it's been good to be single."

Ouch. I knew this. Why did it sting?

It was a reminder I needed. We shouldn't get mixed up with each other again. Life on his own is what he needs right now. We'd had a spontaneous rebound relationship. It was likely we were always doomed to fail. Joel was already cleaning up after me, and I was only here part-time. Now he lived in Phoenix, and I was happy in Paradise Beach. When this week was over, he'd go home.

I tried to change the subject and talked about a new sitcom I'd been watching online.

"It sounds good, want to watch some now?" He stood and slipped out his laptop case from under the desk and set it up on the bed so we could watch it while we worked on the puzzle. We laughed through two episodes, and one particular scene brought tears to our eyes. Joel nearly fell on the floor, he was laughing so hard. He wiped the moisture from his face and his smile had my nerves humming.

His smile made everything seem right with the world.

The noise in the hallway settled down, and we heard someone call out that it was bedtime. The heavy hotel doors swung closed one by one. We watched one more episode to give everyone more time to settle in for the evening and once the credits rolled, I stood up and stretched my arms above my head.

"I'll give sneaking out a try and go home and get some sleep."

"Okay, let me see what the hall looks like." He slipped past me, leaving a tingling sensation where he'd brushed against my arm.

Joel opened the door slowly and peeked out into the dim light. "It's all clear."

I came up behind him and he stepped aside to let me out.

"Well, good night," I whispered, facing him.

"Good night."

We were so close together. It was difficult to tear my eyes from his, but I had to leave. I turned and stepped out into the hallway, and a door several feet away opened. Joel snatched my arm and pulled me back inside. I was wedged in the corner by the door as he closed it as quietly as he could.

"Quick reflexes," I breathed.

He had been concentrating on closing the door quietly, and when he looked over at me, we were both aware of how close our faces were. Emotions were spiraling like a whirlwind. Memories of kissing him haunted me. Our eyes were locked and the key was missing. My body was turning into warm butter. A stray hair fell over his forehead, and I fought the urge to smooth it back into place. His gaze went to my lips and my chest tightened so much. Only a matter of a few inches separated our lips. I could almost hear my heart trying to break out of my rib cage. I breathed in as I moved ever so slightly closer. He touched my arm and inched forward.

A door slammed outside and I jumped, stepping away from Joel.

I faced the bed in the room, pondering what to do if I couldn't sneak out. I could swear he almost kissed me. I couldn't stay here. I turned and whispered, "Maybe, I should try again."

"I didn't hurt you when I grabbed your arm, did I?"

I shook my head—probably too vigorously—as I touched the part of my arm where his fingers had been. "I'm good. Glad you were quick."

"Okay." He refused to look directly at me. "Let me see."

He opened the door again and all was quiet, but before I slipped out, he whispered, "Good night, Lily."

My knees were unsure of themselves. I slipped out without a problem. Once I reached the elevator doors, I hit the button and turned back to see Joel in the doorway watching to see me off.

The doors opened and I gave him a little wave goodbye. Once the doors closed I breathed freely for the first time in a while, muscles letting go of the tension I'd been unconsciously holding.

Chapter Ten

Lily

After spending the afternoon lounging by the pool and watching Joel with his rock-hard abs play water volleyball with his cousins, I tore myself away from the sight and snuck back to my apartment to grab my dress for the reunion. It was a pastel pink with a low sweetheart neckline and an A-line skirt.

Joel wasn't in the room yet, so I took over the bathroom to get ready. I knew he'd cringe seeing my makeup, jewelry, and hair products spread out all over the counter, so once I was satisfied with my hair and makeup, I tossed it all back into the bag I'd hauled it in.

The door lock clicked, and Joel came in just as I was walking out. He froze and stared at me. He stood there in his swim shorts with his chest bare and a towel draped across his shoulders.

"I...uh..." he stammered. "Should get ready."

I had to admit, I enjoyed his labored response. Perhaps this dress looked better on me than I thought.

"You have some time." I vacated the bathroom, careful not to brush up against him as I passed. That would have been too much. I couldn't stop smiling.

I went to sit at the table in front of the puzzle we were working on. We had the outer frame and part of the center completed.

My phone buzzed and I went over to pull it out of my purse, then brought it back to the table. My friend Samantha had texted.

Samantha: I can't wait to see you! Tell me you're coming for sure!!!
Me: I'll be there. With my date.

Texting that was weird, but I didn't want to surprise anyone by walking in with a hot Latino when I'd never mentioned him before.

Samantha: Spill it, girl.
Me: His name is Joel. We've been dating for a while. I didn't want to make a big deal out of it.
Samantha: We need a girls' night so we can catch up on all the deets. I can't wait to meet this guy! Is he treating you well?

I paused. Since I'd been here, Joel had opened every door for me, brought me drinks, and kept asking if I was comfortable. He watched me each night as I left his room to make sure I got to the elevator without being seen. Then there was that moment where I *knew* he was about to kiss me...

Me: 100%

Samantha texted a full line of hearts. Joel was a great guy. Maybe we were better as friends. But that would only work if we kept from almost kissing each other.

Joel came out of the bathroom in a dark suit, with his hair slicked neatly back and my heart jumped. That near-kiss wasn't going to leave my mind any time soon.

He was working on tying a pastel pink tie. He'd found the perfect color.

"Ready?" he asked, slipping his hands in his pockets and watching me.

"Uh..." I struggled.

What did he ask me again?

"Okay," I finally said.

"Let's do this." I jumped up and hurried past the bed, past him, and rushed to the door. I didn't want to change my mind about going. And my mind was growing fuzzier the longer I sat and stared at him.

Soon we were heading down the elevator and to the parking garage. Joel had let his family know we'd be out for the evening, and he said he'd only gotten encouragement, especially from Abuela, who was delighted he was taking me on a date.

I drove my car and it took a little over an hour to get to San Diego. My old high school in the suburb where I grew up largely hadn't changed. Freshly painted red letters spelling Franklin High were above the front entrance. The double doors were propped open and people were filtering in from the parking lot. Couples dressed up and walking hand and hand created a steady stream inside the building.

"Here we are." I breathed in and out slowly. Most of my memories here were positive. I loved my friends, and back then Alex had seemed so perfect.

"Are you ready for this?"

I nodded even though my stomach began to ache. Doubts swarmed all over me. It may not be the best idea to bring a fake date, but I didn't want to let my stupid ex keep me from having a good time with my friends.

Joel walked around the front of the car and opened the driver's side door for me. I finally took off my seatbelt and accepted his out-stretched hand. Warmth spread from my fingers to my chest as he helped me up.

"You look beautiful this evening," he said softly.

My heart fluttered. "So do you."

I took his arm and followed the queue going inside.

Past the doorway, a large poster was set on an easel, reading Franklin High Reunion Class of 2013 in red and black, glitter-covered letters.

We checked in at a table with a sweet older woman with large heart-shaped glasses and then were directed to the gym down the hall (in case students somehow forgot where it was after ten years).

The gym was decorated with white balloons and streamers in two different shades of blue. A buffet table of snacks and treats was set up along one wall, and round tables with white tablecloths were spread around the room with tealight candle centerpieces. A young man with long blond hair wearing a Pink Floyd T-shirt and baggy jeans managed a table filled with DJ equipment. Large speakers on the stage floor blasted out the Aerosmith song from the movie where the astronauts saved the world. A large open space on the floor below it allowed for dancing.

We filtered in with others who were finding tables and settling down. Some of the former cheerleaders I recognized were squealing and hugging. Scanning the room, I didn't see Samantha or Eliza yet.

We wandered over to an empty table and Joel pulled out a chair for me. "I'm sorry, I need to use the restroom, but when I come back, would you like some punch?"

"Sure." I nodded. "Thanks."

Once he left, I glanced to my left and spotted someone who definitely did not belong here.

My sister.

And Alex.

My sister was HOLDING HANDS with my ex.

Dana's golden hair fell in perfect waves around her shoulders. Her strapless black dress hugged her tiny figure, and matching stilettos pushed her up to stand about an inch taller than Alex. Alex's dark hair sported a new, loose perm and he smiled with his lips tightly together. Dana spotted me and she smiled and waved like she was in a beauty pageant.

What. The. Actual. Hell?

Alex looked as if he'd swallowed something the wrong way and he began to cough uncontrollably.

Dana patted him on the back for a few seconds, then dragged him over toward me still hacking.

There I stood, not knowing what to do.

"Hi, Lily," Dana said, dropping Alex's hand once they were directly in front of me. "I didn't mean for this to be awkward or anything."

Why would this be awkward? Surely it was natural to want to date the man who cheated on your sister, right?

Natural for the insane.

Alex gained control of himself and took a step back when I shot him a look that I hoped reflected how I felt to see him.

"Alex and I ran into each other at Smoothie Heaven," Dana said, twirling a lock of her hair. "We got to talking and one thing led to another. When I heard about this reunion, I just couldn't let him go alone."

My mouth went as dry as the muffins Dana burnt the last time she tried to bake. "You're *dating*?"

"We just make sense, don't you think?" Dana shrugged.

"No." I paused, shaking my head. "Actually, yes. So much yes. You two are perfect for each other."

Alex stepped behind Dana, refusing to meet my eyes. Which was a shame, because I was trying to make lasers shoot from my eyes.

"We are, aren't we? I'm quite good at making time for relationships." Dana didn't even catch my sarcasm. "It's important that the other person feels seen and heard and made time for. I always do that. I really should have been a life coach, because everyone comes to me for advice."

Last year she'd told me all about how I could have saved my relationship with Alex if I'd only been a little less...myself.

I folded my arms, contemplating whether to try to make her see how outrageous this all was or simply walk away.

"What happened to that woman you went on the cruise with?" I couldn't resist asking him.

"Uh..." I could only see about half of him behind Dana. He scratched the back of his neck. Was this guilt?

"She was all wrong for him," Dana asserted, sliding a finger across her gold necklace. "She treated him so badly. *I* know how to treat a man. You should let me teach you, Lily." She circled a finger in the air, aiming toward my head. "You could also use a good trip to my stylist to do something about how flat your hair is, maybe add some highlights and extensions. And you *have* to try this new diet I'm on."

Gah.

"It's a kale smoothie each morning and it could do wonders for your dull skin. Look how mine is glowing." She patted her cheeks. "Men love that. I'd *love* to help you."

I was sure she would. I wasn't interested in any of her 'help'.

"No, thanks. I'm fine." My arms were still folded and I realized I was digging my nails into my upper arms. I relaxed then, taking in a cleansing breath, knowing I'd need it. Dana wasn't done. If anything, she was just warming up.

"I've been helping Mom redecorate their condo," she said, ignoring me and staying in her world. "She raved about how my skin glows. Have you talked to her lately? She hasn't been answering my texts promptly. Alex always texts me back right away. He's so considerate." She finally took a breath and fanned her face. "Excuse me, I am feeling a bit dizzy. I believe I'm a little dehydrated."

Alex took her by the arm. "Let's get you something to drink."

I spotted Joel walking over with two cups of punch. His timing couldn't have been better. "Speaking of considerate men, I met a guy who I couldn't let go. Let me introduce you to my boyfriend."

Dana's eyes sprang wide, "What did you say? Perhaps I'm more dehydrated than I thought."

Joel locked eyes with me, and I could practically see question marks in his eyes. He set the punch down on the table and then stood beside me. I hoped he saw my desperation.

"Darling, I'm sorry I took so long." He slipped his arm around my waist, then he leaned down and gently pressed his lips against mine. His kiss was soft and tender, melting my muscles and disarming me completely.

He pulled away too quickly, leaving my lips buzzing and legs needing support. I leaned into his side as he gave my sister a winning smile.

Dana folded her arms and eyed me suspiciously as she pointed at Joel. "There's something familiar about you."

He offered her his hand and she simply stared at it. "Joel Velásquez. We met briefly at Amy and Kyle's wedding last year."

"Oh. Right." She poked Alex and said, "I need something to drink, remember?"

Alex was giving Joel the stink eye as he allowed Dana to lead him away.

I breathed in and out very slowly then turned to face Joel.

Chapter Eleven

Joel

I was playing a dutiful boyfriend here. That was my role. But that brief kiss left me wanting more. It wasn't good.

"I guess you remember my sister Dana." Lily wrapped her arms around her chest and squeezed herself tightly.

The only other time I'd spoken to Dana had been at Kyle and Amy's wedding. It wasn't even a full conversation.

Lily was looking at me as if she were about to give me the news of something tragic. "And that was Alex."

"That was Alex?" The jerk who cheated on Lily? If only I were a caveman with a big club and no sense of civility.

"I'm so sorry I dragged you into my drama."

I wrapped my arms around her and pulled her against me.

"Hey, don't worry about me. Are you okay? Do you want to leave?"

She shook her head against my chest as I held her close. "I don't want them to think they've bothered me. Dana never told me she was dating him. She wasn't supposed to be here at all. This isn't her reunion."

I rubbed her back, my heart doing somersaults. I worried she might hear it. But I didn't want to let go of her. My heart was convinced she belonged here, but my brain reminded me it wouldn't last.

I couldn't imagine what it would be like to be in her position.

"Do you want something to eat?" I offered, stroking her soft hair.

"Yes. Did they have anything chocolate over there?" She nodded her chin toward the snack table.

"I don't want to leave you alone again. Why don't you come with me?" I reluctantly stepped back, took her hand, and led her over to the table. I handed her a plate and watched her as she wandered past several types of cookies, then caught up with her as she took a brownie from a tray. She added three more to her plate.

I wanted to cringe at the amount of chocolate. But didn't want to show her I had any opinion on it. She was clearly upset. I was never great at catching her hints in the past, or at listening when she needed me to. She used to say I was too critical, and I was determined to do better. If she wanted to talk, I wanted to be there with whatever she needed. No unwanted advice.

We made our way back to the table and once we sat down, she sipped on her punch, and I watched Dana and Alex slowly dance across the room.

I watched her silently for a few moments and waited while she ate. I watched her pause and take several deep breaths, and I reached over to rub her shoulder.

"I'm here if you want to talk."

"Thank you," she said, and our eyes locked. "This was harder than I thought."

I took her hand and squeezed it. It fit so naturally in mine.

"This night can't get any worse right?" Her lips twisted in a half smile.

"Likely not worse than that."

"I just want to have fun tonight and not think about this crap anymore."

"You deserve to, Lily. Tell me what I can do to help."

She glanced at the dance floor, then back at me. "Do you want to dance?"

Dana and Alex were still dancing, but not really. It was mostly hugging with a little swaying. I couldn't believe the nerve of that guy, coming tonight with her sister and blindsiding her like that. Why didn't they just leave? Lily didn't deserve any of this. She'd said she wanted a fun night with her friends and I wanted to give that to her. "Sure."

Lily gave me a small, sly grin. "Should we request something we can salsa to?"

"Absolutely we should. I'll be right back."

I hopped up and went to chat with the DJ, then hurried back. I found Lily once again with company, but this time she wore her beautiful smile that was like butterflies in the sun.

She stepped out of a group hug with two women around her age.

"Gals, this is my date, Joel Velásquez." Lily slipped her arm around me and patted my chest. "Joel, these are my best friends, Samantha Bell and Eliza Hailey."

"Very nice to meet you both," I said, offering my free hand.

"Nice to meet you as well," Samantha said reaching out to shake my hand. She was a little taller than Eliza and Lily, but perhaps it was only her hot pink shoes that matched her long, flowy dress.

"You have a date!" Eliza's eyes brightened as she adjusted her large black-rimmed glasses. Her dark hair was twisted up behind her head and she wore a simple black skirt with a sparkly top. "Samantha and I are dateless, except for each other."

"Yeah, all bets are off if I get a better offer from Jimmy Song over there." Samantha jerked her head toward the tall, dark-haired man wearing a bright red tie a few tables over.

"Oh, please. He'll only do because Samantha's high school crush isn't here."

"Should I have invited Chris tonight?" Lily wagged her eyebrows at her friend and then turned to me. "Samantha was completely lovestruck by my cousin Chris in high school, but he graduated a few years before we did so this isn't his class."

"I see," I said. "I've only recently met him, but he seems like a great guy."

"That was a long time ago." Samantha blushed and narrowed her eyes at her friends. "It was also a *secret*."

"I've never told him a thing," Lily asserted. "He's the assistant manager at the hotel now. And single."

"Maybe you should go down and stay at the resort some time and check him out." Eliza held her clutch with both hands and bumped Samantha with her shoulder.

"The next song will be for us," I whispered in Lily's ear, loving the nearness and the sweet scent of her perfume.

A lively Latin tune sounded up and I dropped my arm from around Lily and slipped my hand in hers again.

"If you'll excuse us for a moment, Ladies," I said to her friends.

As we were leaving, Eliza mouthed to Lily what I was pretty sure was, "He's gorgeous."

I was flattered, of course. Was it that extra time I'd spent on my hair? Or the cut of my suit? *Don't let this go to your head, man.*

Hopefully, Alex was realizing Lily deserved so much better than him. It was a strange comfort to know Lily's sister would very likely torment him. I had no respect for cheaters in any form. I couldn't understand why he hadn't been able to cherish what he'd had when Lily was with him.

My heart twisted, remembering the pain of losing her. I pushed it aside and led her to the dance floor.

I slipped my arm around her shoulder, and she linked her right hand with my left, sparking electricity. My feet took over moving with the music. She remembered everything I'd taught her, moving her hips and feet in perfect harmony. Salsa was a lively dance, and my partner was hot enough to burn a line in the floor. I thought my heart would ignite and turn to flames, then be nothing but a pile of steaming ashes when she was done with me.

On the final note of the song, I spun her and dipped her, and held her there for a few amazing seconds as the music died away. My breath was heavy as I held her gaze then pulled her back up. She stumbled and I pulled her against my chest. She held me like a life raft, her face so close to mine. I stared at her enticing red lips.

I think I would have kissed her again if she hadn't stepped back when a new song began. It was an electronic rhythm and she rocked with the beat. I tried to dance along, but my brain was out to lunch. This woman was amazing. Her laugh. Her smile.

Everything about the way she moved made me want more.

How did she have this effect on me?

She was a little too far away now. The music escalated to a big finish, and I took her in my arms, spun her around, and lowered her in another dip. Her lips were inches away, her eyes went to mine...then she kissed me.

She slipped her arm around my neck and slid her fingers into my hair.

I was hungry and eager, but as I tried to force myself to slow down, she didn't let me. My heartbeat took off, and the sensation sent quivers down my spine. Something was sparking between us, and it was about to catch fire. I kissed her eagerly, needing her to be closer. She held me even tighter and let out a soft moan.

I slid my hands up and down her back. I didn't want to let go and she showed no signs of releasing me.

My earlier kiss may have been for show, but this one was real. And it was molten lava. Hobbits could throw a ring at us at any moment.

She clung to me as if she'd fly off into space if she let go.

Another song came on, and I was vaguely aware of a tap on my shoulder.

"People are starting to stare. You should take this outside so you don't embarrass me."

I turned around to see Dana, standing with her hand on one hip jutted to the side, rolling her eyes.

Lily pulled back from me, and my mouth was buzzing. We were both out of breath, both from the dance with our feet and our lips.

Lily blinked. "We did get a little carried away, didn't we? Good luck with Alex, you'll need it."

She slipped her arm through mine and we walked back to our table. Eliza and Samantha were there sipping on drinks.

I wondered if they'd seen that kiss.

That kiss.

It was like we'd been swept up in a mini tornado.

We were seriously blurring the lines.

Chapter Twelve

Lily

E *at your heart out, Alex.* Jagger had nothing on Joel when he moved his body to the beat. My heart did an impression of an Olympic gymnast the entire dance, and I couldn't take my eyes off him. The man was a walking distraction. It was like we were picking up from where we left off with that sizzling kiss that could've set off sparklers. I hadn't meant it to do that. I was caught up in the magic and emotion of the dance. When he dipped me low, I was a goner. By all accounts, he was into it as much as I was. I swear it was epic, movie-worthy material.

But what if he thought it was part of the act? It was mind-blowing, glass-shattering...and I didn't even know what else, but it brought back so many of the feelings that had hit me so hard and fast when we first met.

On the way back to our table, I saw some other friends I hadn't seen since high school. They loved meeting Joel, and I loved introducing him. This was the wonderful thing about reunions, catching up with people you once loved and lost touch with.

I was doing the same thing with Joel this week in secret.

When we went back to our table, we were alone for a few moments in silence. Neither one of us seemed to know what to say.

"I'll go get us some water," Joel said, placing his hand on the back of my chair as he stood up.

"Thanks."

When Samantha and Eliza came back to the table, they both had stories of the men they'd danced with.

"But what I want to know…" Eliza said, leaning forward over the table on her elbows. "Are you going to marry this guy?"

Samantha nodded in agreement. "You should marry him. The way he dances…"

"You seem into him in a big way." Eliza wiggled her eyebrows.

"Oh…I…" Luckily, Joel returned with a plastic cup of water for me. I took it and gulped it down so I wouldn't have to speak.

"So," Joel said, eyeing me sideways. "How did you three meet? Were you in the same class?"

"We were all in the school choir," Eliza told Joel. "But Lily was the best."

"I was only in for the first year though." Samantha took another sip of her punch. "I joined the girl's volleyball team."

"But we've been best friends since Freshman year," Eliza said. She wagged a finger at the two of us. "How'd you two meet?"

"At my cousin Amy's wedding in Las Vegas." No need to go further than that.

"I love weddings," Samantha said, setting her cup down. "I've been trying to get someone to let me cater one."

"You're a caterer?" Joel asked.

"Not quite." She shook her head. "Right now I'm a sous chef at a local Italian restaurant."

"She's very talented," I told Joel.

"I don't doubt it." Joel glanced at me, then focused on Eliza. "And what do you do?"

"I'm working at the Birch Aquarium in La Jolla. I'm also finishing a Master's in Marine Biology."

"Wow, cool." Joel was hooked when she talked about getting to work with sea lions.

I was too busy watching his smiling face to follow. There were little lines around his eyes. He had to be tired. We'd done a lot of dancing, but I wasn't ready for the evening to end yet. Once we got out of here, would we need to have a conversation about all the kissing?

They both wanted to know about Joel's job and even though it wasn't an exciting one, they both paid close attention.

Very close attention. Were they studying him?

If they were worried about another Alex situation, that would never be Joel. I knew it in my soul. When our thirty-day trial had ended, I'd been the one to walk away, not him.

A cute guy in a blue-collar shirt asked Eliza to dance, and she jumped up to accept.

"Well then," Samantha said, standing and smoothing down her dress. "I'll go see if I can find another partner for myself."

"Go for it," I encouraged.

Joel pointed out that the DJ on the stage had left, and now a young woman was controlling the music. She had a black tattoo across her neck like a choker necklace.

"That looks painful," I said, clutching my neck. "That tattoo."

"You still against tattoos?" he asked me with a sideways smile.

"Not tattoos," I corrected, raising a finger in the air. "Needles."

"Ah. No one *likes* needles."

"No, seamstresses like them. They have to or the world doesn't make sense."

"Good thing you're a musician then." Joel grinned.

"I won't say teaching high schoolers is always a picnic, but my choir students are usually always happy to come to practice. Maybe they love music like I do," I said, shrugging, "or they're just happy it's not math."

Joel chuckled and raised his water glass to mine. We tapped our plastic cups together as the DJ started a new song. I didn't realize I was mouthing the lyrics until Joel joined in, silently singing. He added some drama, clutching the center of his chest in both hands and closing his eyes as he pretended to belt out the long high note Celine Dion was singing.

"I had no idea you could sing like that," I teased.

He opened his eyes and grinned at me. "I have many hidden talents. I can also pretend I know karate and fall on my face trying to do that crane move from *Karate Kid*."

"I *have* to see that. Immediately."

"No one should be allowed to see that." He rubbed the back of his neck. "I tried to convince my friends it was easy and I stood on a chair to demonstrate. But I haven't tried since I was a teenager, so maybe I'm awesome at it now. Who knows?"

"Ah, I bet I could fall even more spectacularly than you."

"Maybe we should try skydiving. It's all about falling, right?"

"I would hope there would at least be a required class. But I'll still give that a hard pass."

We chatted the night away, and before we left, Samantha whispered to me, "You better keep this guy, he's so fun. And that kiss on the dance floor had me blushing."

My face burned thinking about it. At the moment nothing else mattered, but it was so insanely public.

When we headed back to the car, I told him he could have a turn driving. I didn't want to bring up the kiss, but I wanted to know how he felt about it.

He opened the car door for me and instead of getting in, I faced him and leaned back against the car.

"That was quite a show we put on, eh?" I wanted him to push back and admit it wasn't all for show. I watched his eyes, searching for clues.

"Yeah," he said when he finally spoke. "Alex was probably kicking himself that he'd lost you."

But that's not all it was. Why was it so hard to come out and say what I wanted to? *I kissed you for real because I couldn't help it.*

We'd gone down this road before. This arrangement was temporary. He'd go back to Phoenix soon and I didn't know if we'd ever see each other again.

I was helping him out, so he was helping me.

We didn't talk about our kiss anymore on the drive back to Paradise Beach, but we talked about nearly everything else.

The sun was down but the interstate was bright with street lights and red tail lights from the cars ahead of us.

"Did you have any fun traditions with your extended family growing up?" Joel asked.

When we were first together, I'd kept talking about my family to a bare minimum. He'd met my sister, so I thought he understood why.

"Not really. If you remember, my dad has one sister, my Aunt Lillian."

"Amy's mother, right?"

"Right. My mom didn't like my father's family, so I went to see them in Las Vegas several times when I was young with just my Dad. My mom has two brothers and she isn't close with them. I don't know them well at all. I used to go to my grandmother's house after school because my parents always worked late. Mom worked in an art studio and Dad was an architect. Grandma taught me how to play piano."

"I'd like to have met her. I bet she was wonderful."

"She was. When she died a few years ago I wasn't able to be with her." I took in a deep breath with the stabbing memory and blinked back tears. "I wasn't about to let you miss out on saying goodbye to yours."

"I appreciate that, Lily." His voice was low and tender. "I'm sorry my grandmother's scare brought up difficult memories. If it had truly been her final moments, she would have passed on delighted to have met you." His jaw went tight for a few seconds, then he said, "I'm a creep for lying to her."

"I know you've never liked messing up. You're always hard on yourself."

He leaned his left elbow on the door and glanced at me, then turned back to the view of the cars ahead. The six-lane highway had decreased to two.

"I've never liked disappointing people."

"Is this about being the so-called 'miracle child'?" He hadn't mentioned that until recently.

"Gah." He wrinkled his nose and gripped the steering wheel tighter. I hate that. I was babied quite a bit when I was younger. Being a perfectionist at work can be a good thing, but in my personal life not so much. It was one of the reasons Kim cited when she rejected my proposal."

"She gave you a list of reasons?"

"Pretty much." He shifted uncomfortably in his seat. "It was item-ized, alphabetized, and color-coded."

"Yikes. All you told me last year was that she said no. Something about her wanting to go in a new direction. This is far more interesting. That's actually what I'd picture *you* doing to refuse someone." I poked his shoulder.

He let out a quick, sharp laugh. "I've never broken up with anyone that way, thank you very much."

"I'm sorry. I'm sorry things didn't work out with Kim, but she sounds like a perfectionist too."

"Probably."

"The truth is, I hate disappointing people too. My mother means well, but she gets involved so much in my life. And my sister is more complicated. We were friends when we were little, but now she's always disappointed with me. And she really disregarded my feelings dating my ex."

"You held your own tonight with your sister. How do you feel about it?"

"I supposed I feel down." I folded my arms and stared out the window at the dark trees whizzing by. "The biggest reason I moved out of San Diego was to distance myself from my family. I feel guilty for feeling this way."

"I'm sure I'd feel the same way."

I shook my head. "Enough about my family. Let's talk more about yours. Tell me something you did with them growing up that you haven't mentioned."

He thought for a moment, twisting his lips.

"Hmm...Every Sunday when I was growing up, my family would gather for a family dinner," Joel said, eyes on the road and his hands perfectly placed at ten and two on the steering wheel. "Once when it was at Tía Juanita's house, she had little trash bags filled with water hanging from her ceiling."

"What? Why?"

"She said she was having a problem with fruit flies and she thought this would make them go away. But it turned out to be a good way to get rid of her company. My cousin Carlos thought it would be funny to poke tiny holes in the ones over the dining room table. You can probably guess what happened when we sat down to eat."

"Wow."

"They were tiny holes, but we still got wet. And the flies didn't go anywhere."

I laughed so hard, picturing what Juanita's face must have looked like.

"It sounds like Carlos was on their list long before he got a divorce."

"He was always the troublemaker."

"Ah, and you were the miracle kid. I see where this is going."

"I feel like you're trying to psychoanalyze me."

"Sorry. I was only making an observation. It sounds like not wanting to disappoint your family, or letting them know you screw up as any human does, might go back a long way."

"I suppose...maybe we should talk about your family more."

"They're a hot, steaming mess. But to their credit, I will say they've never tried to rid the house of flies with bags of water."

"I'd like someone to psychoanalyze Tía Juanita."

"That could be interesting. I've never met anyone so superstitious."

"I wish I could say the same, but my late Tía Marisol was just as bad. She thought rubbing chicken poop in her hair would stop it from falling out."

"You're kidding, right?"

"If you only knew how much I wish I was. It's the reason she wanted to raise her own chickens."

"Your family is so entertaining, Joel."

"Don't you mean in need of intervention?"

"We all need that at some point, but some of us are more fun than others."

"I've had fun with you tonight, Lily."

"Me too." I held back again from what I really wanted to ask. *Was the most fun of the night when we kissed in front of everyone? Twice?*

At least the awkwardness had passed. Before we reached the hotel, we stopped at a grocery store nearby and grabbed some more slices of cake to test out. Instead of leaving after we found the cake, we wandered the aisles of the store and snagged some snacks for the hotel. Before we were done, someone announced over the PA system that the store was closing. We made a mad dash for the popcorn aisle and Joel sped up the cart heading toward the front of the store, then hopped on the bottom of the cart with both feet. He wore a huge smile as he sailed into the checkout line like a silly teenager.

The *actual* teenager manning the register cracked up as we quickly emptied the cart.

"I wish they'd let me do that," the teen said, dragging our items over the scanner one by one.

"We won't tell if you do," I whispered.

Once we reached the hotel, we emptied the bags and decided we had enough food to stay for days. I pulled out the box of microwave popcorn and took out one of the bags.

"Want to see what there is on TV?"

"There's a movie on tonight you might like. Do you trust me?" Joel asked, striking a serious tone and eyeing me without blinking.

"Yes," I said without hesitation. "I do."

I woke in the morning to the sight of a wall of pillows. I was on top of the comforter, in the bed. The extra blanket from the closet was on top of me. I propped myself up on my elbow and peeked over the pillow wall we'd made last night to watch TV.

Joel was fast asleep on his side. He was so peaceful. I had a mad urge to kiss him on the cheek.

My throat clenched.

This was a bad idea.

The TV was still on, playing a morning news show. We'd talked late into the night then watched a movie. And here we were still.

"We're adults," he'd said.

"With one bed in the room," I'd responded. "And one bad history."

"It's a king-size, there's plenty of room." He'd stacked all the pillows in the room in the center of the bed, then took the extra ones down from the closet. "How's this?"

I'd stared at the pillow wall. One of my favorite movies had been about to come on, and I'd had mere minutes to decide.

Wasn't it harmless? If I sat on the edge with a pillow barrier between us?

I'd sat down gingerly on the edge. Then so did he. And there we were in the same bed again, but with what was hopefully a safe distance and all the pillows.

Naturally, I did the awkward thing and fell asleep.

I hadn't meant to stay overnight, but this certainly simplified things. I hadn't had to sneak out or back in. I carefully moved out of bed and went to the bathroom. I cringed at my face in the mirror. My makeup was smudged and my hair was insane. I looked like a raccoon coming back from a rave. I tiptoed back out to grab my makeup bag and Joel stirred. I snatched the bag and ran back to the bathroom. I couldn't let him see me like this.

"Lily? Are you okay?" He called out sleepily.

I cracked the door. "I'm fine. Go back to sleep."

"I can't. We're supposed to meet everyone downstairs for breakfast, remember?"

"Okay. I'll be out in a few." I locked the door and got to work scrubbing my face clean and reapplying fresh makeup.

My sundress from yesterday was wrinkled. I wish I'd thought to grab a new outfit before running in here.

I came out of the bathroom slowly and made a loud announcement. "I'm coming out!"

"I'm dressed. Didn't you see?"

"I didn't want to chance it. In case you decided to change out here." I continued out to where he was and he laughed, scratching the morning stubble on his chin. "I don't sleep or walk around naked. And I promise to change in the bathroom. Okay?"

"Good."

I seriously needed to get the idea of him walking around naked out of my head.

His hair was askew, and I wanted more than anything to put my fingers through it and smooth it down. My pulse was doing an impression of a roadrunner.

"Why didn't you wake me up last night?" I sat down in the desk chair and shifted it to face him.

"You seemed so tired, I didn't want to disturb you." He got up, walked over to the dresser, and pulled some clothes out of a drawer. The gym shorts he'd slept in were ridiculously hot. "You're welcome to stay again tonight if it's easier for you."

Breathing was difficult. I didn't know what to say. Perhaps it would be easier, but it could also be much harder. Sharing a room with him was giving me thoughts I'd rather not have. I remembered all too well our time together last summer. The whirlwind of ups and downs. The feelings I had then were confusing. I both needed him but at the same time, felt I wasn't good enough.

With all my other issues, the top priority right now needed to be to stop staring at the way he looked in his shorts.

Chapter Thirteen
Joel

A cheery gentleman in khaki shorts and a red polo shirt greeted us at the end of the dock by a pair of blue pontoon boats. "Welcome, everyone. We're boarding now, so find a good seat." He waved us to the nearest boat.

My family was too large for one boat, so others were directed to the second one. Some families had opted to stay on the beach that morning instead.

I held Lily's hand as she stepped down into the boat, then we both helped Abuela ease down to the deck.

Abuela wore a red sunhat tied under her chin and a matching dress. She was beaming with delight. I would have rather been with Lily and Abuela on the boat with more of my cousins, instead of with my parents, tías, and tíos. Despite how I loved them, they had far too much to say.

As we all took a seat, I couldn't hold back a yawn. Lily and I had stayed up late watching a comedy movie I knew she'd love. I'm glad I was right. She'd said she was still surprised at how much I remembered about her. Did she think when she'd left that I'd erase her from my mind completely? She thought so little of herself and her impact on my life. In her family, she was frequently forgotten about. I told her I never would.

I completely lost my head last evening. It was buzzing after she kissed me in front of her ex. Between our dance and her smile that made me want to give her everything I own, I lost control and kissed her again.

Nothing about her was forgettable.

But the other thing I couldn't forget was the way I crumbled after our thirty days were over and she simply gave up.

Kim had given me a plethora of reasons she was walking away, and Lily just left after our last fight. I'd wanted to forget, but it wasn't possible. It didn't matter how many times I told myself we made a mistake getting married so fast, or that we were simply a rebound. I was still left alone with half of my heart. I had to push it from my mind.

She was here now like a beautiful dream sitting next to me. She wore a light pink sundress over a purple bathing suit and a large-brimmed straw hat that made it difficult to sit too close.

Abuela sat on my other side and patted my cheek. "I'm so excited."

"Me too." I bent down and kissed her soft cheek.

"But why do we need a boat to look at dolphins?" Dad asked from his seat on the bench across from us. He took off his baseball cap and scratched his thinning gray hair. "We can see them when we're fishing on the pier."

"There is more to life than fishing, Armando," Mom spat as she fanned herself with the dolphin cruise brochure. Her face was beginning to match the rosy color of her floral-patterned dress. "Yet it is all you talk about," she continued, sneering at Dad. "We aren't here for you to fish."

"I do love fresh fish," Abuela said, folding her arms. "Let Armando bring us some fish."

"We have nowhere to cook fish, Mamá," Mom told her.

"What if we build a bonfire on the beach?" Tío Mateo suggested.

"Stop encouraging this," Mom insisted, facing her brother. "I'm trying to get Armando to cut back on fishing."

"Why do I need to when we're here at the beach?" Dad's eyes widened as he gestured out to the water.

"We are here to celebrate Mamá's birthday." Mom's tone was sharp and firm. "You need to spend time with the family."

"I *will be* spending time with family. Mateo, Pedro, and Andreas"—Dad held out a finger for each name—"Javier, Diego. They all said they'd go."

My tíos looked away, not wanting to get on Mom's bad side.

"Let the boys have fun, Eva," Abuela said, then shifted to the side to gaze around at the water. "It's so beautiful out here." She turned back toward the dock. "When is this tour starting?"

Another gentleman in a red polo shirt arrived on the dock and stepped into our boat. This guy had long blond hair, large sunglasses, and a white baseball cap he wore backwards. He started up the boat motor and shouted over the roar. "Good morning! My name is Shawn and I'll be your guide today. Please secure your valuables, it will be quite windy when we get going. You'll find lifejackets stored below your seat." He stepped to the middle of the boat and pointed to the bench seats we sat on. "They're required by California law, and I'll be happy to assist you if you need help putting them on. We'll be making a few stops in places where it will be optional to get out and swim."

We all stood and pulled out the lifejackets under the bench seats.

"Does anyone need help?" Shawn said.

"Do you need help, Abuela?" I held out an orange vest for her.

"Nonsense, let me have that." She took it from me and strapped herself into it.

Lily took hers and put it on, then pulled her camera out of her bag and threw the strap around her neck.

Shawn adjusted his glasses and took a seat in the white leather chair behind the helm at the boat's midpoint.

"It is illegal to swim with wild dolphins, so we don't get out if we see them in the place we normally swim. If you happen to see a dolphin swim by while you're in the water, you must keep your distance. Do not touch, attempt to interact with, or harass them."

Tía Carmen on the other side of Abuela hissed at her husband. "Pedro, did you hear that? No harassing the dolphins."

"Why on earth would I harass a dolphin?" Tío Pedro looked as if someone had just slapped him in the face.

"It is *exactly* the kind of thing you would do. You're always playing pranks."

"With the kids, Carmen, not wild animals." Pedro rolled his eyes and leaned his arm on the side of the boat. "Aye, aye, aye."

Tía Carmen clicked her teeth. "Keep your hands to yourself if you go swimming."

Lily glanced at me and I shrugged. I honestly didn't know what Tía Carmen was upset about. Tío Pedro loved pranks, yes, but the only ones I'd seen had involved things like putting saltwater in my cousin Javier's water bottle or photobombing Rosa's photos.

"We'll be cruising by places we typically view dolphins," Shawn announced. "We cannot make any guarantees about their whereabouts. Does anyone have any questions?"

"How strong is the wind?" Tía Juanita asked from her seat next to Mom. Juanita's husband, Tío Andreas shook his head.

"Your hat has a chin strap, you'll be fine," he said.

"Not if the wind is at hurricane speed." Tía Juanita tightened her strap.

"We won't be traveling anywhere approaching that fast," Shawn assured them. "We cruise around 35 to 40 miles per hour."

"Oh, that is too fast," Tía Carmen complained, eyes going wide.

"Make your speed an even number for luck," Tía Juanita told Shawn with a sharp nod.

"I will see what I can do," Shawn said.

"At this point, we may never leave the dock," I whispered to Lily. She was trying to keep from laughing.

"You mean the tour isn't sitting here watching your family?"

"It's always possible a dolphin may cruise past us."

"I'm ready in case we do leave the dock." Lily held up her camera in front of me and I smiled as she snapped a shot.

The boat jerked away from the dock and we cruised at turtle speed toward the open water. The noise of the motor revving up to speed drowned out any further issues anyone had.

The water was a cool blue, shining bright in the sun. The waves bounced up and down in front of us as the boat sliced the water and stirred up sea foam.

I held onto my baseball hat and put my arm around Lily. We went at top speed for a bit and the wind slapped our faces. It was certainly not the seventy-plus miles an hour needed to qualify as "hurricane speed".

Shawn slowed the boat down and we bounced up and down in the wake as we shifted to moving at a crawl. "Point your cameras over to your right, here they come."

A pod of dolphins was many yards off, visible only by their shiny gray dorsal fins.

Everyone jumped to their feet, but I sat and put my arm around Abuela as she turned to see.

"Beautiful," she whispered with a delightful smile on her beautifully wrinkled face.

"This is a pod of bottlenose dolphins." Shawn pointed in their direction, still holding onto the helm with his other hand. "They are very social creatures. They hunt together and teach each other tricks for catching food."

Lily snapped several photos. "I'm sure Rosa will get even better shots."

Rosa was on the boat behind us which was slowing down as well.

"She'll probably want photos from you too." I wanted Lily to believe in herself. She was always better than she thought she was.

The dolphins moved farther out to sea so we cruised on. Lily sat close to me again, and I wrapped my arm around her shoulders automatically. It was becoming far too natural.

Once the boat ferried up to a small island, Shawn slowed us down to a halt and dropped the anchor. The second boat parked beside us. "You can see a few dolphins farther out there," he said, pointing behind us. "But anyone who wants to get in the water here is welcome to."

My family largely refused. Lily and I were the youngest people on this boat, and no one seemed interested.

Some of my cousins jumped in the water from the other pontoon.

Lily asked if I wanted to get in. I wasn't sure. I loved swimming, but it was always in clean, sanitary swimming pools where you could clearly see the bottom. The ocean held much more mystery...and wildlife. "I don't know."

"Didn't you wear your swim shorts for a reason?" Lily tapped on my thigh and my skin buzzed.

"Well..."

"I haven't been able to convince Mamá to let me take her in for her yearly mammogram," Tía Carmen said, unnecessarily loud.

"I'm right here, Carmen." Abuela rolled her eyes. "I've lived this long, and I'm not dead from cancer yet."

"Mamá!" Tía Juanita looked as if Abuela had just announced she was joining the space program and traveling to the moon. "Are you saying you never go?"

"Nope," Abulea said, shaking her head.

This wasn't good.

"I go every year, like clockwork," Tía Carmen said. She eyed Abuela sternly. "You have to go every year."

"Yes, you do, Mamá," Tía Juanita said. "Early detection is the only way to go. Listen to Carmen. You *have* to go. Are you afraid? It's only a little squish." Juanita lifted her hands over her chest and pressed her palms together to illustrate. "It's not bad."

My Dad dragged a hand down over his face, Tío Pedro looked as if someone had just told him he needed to perform an exorcism. Tío Andreas kept his eyes on the ocean.

"Don't call it a squish." Carmen leaned forward and narrowed her eyes at Juanita then turned back to Abuela. "It's uncomfortable, but not painful. Yes, I'll be honest and say it's awkward, but the tech is always so nice. She shows you what to do and puts your breast in the machine and then–"

"I'm not interested in being pressed like a grape," Abuela announced. "Look at me," she gestured to her chest. "Is there even enough here to worry about?"

Oh boy. Time to jump into the ocean.

My tías were chiding Abuela and I turned to Lily, dropping my arm from around her and taking her hand. "Okay, let's get in the water."

Now I wished we'd brought scuba gear so we'd be sure to be even farther away from this conversation.

She smiled brighter than the sunlight all around us and pulled off her sundress to reveal the rest of her purple bikini. From her long legs to her curves, I struggled to look away.

Yep. Time to jump into some cold water.

I pulled off my shirt and followed Lily to the back of the boat where there was a little door to open and a step down to the water. I jumped in, plunging under the water. The cold blast shocked all my senses. It was exactly what I needed.

I popped back up for air and watched Lily step off the edge while keeping her legs close together as she jumped to make a smaller splash.

When she came back up, her wet hair was flat against her head. She tilted her head to the side, then took off to swim in that direction away from the boat.

I followed her, and once we were several yards from the boat, she came to a stop and faced me as she moved her hands back and forth in the water.

My anxiety about the mysteries beneath us was gone. Everything about being with her felt right.

"I feel like I should apologize for my family. Again."

"You don't need to." She giggled. "Older people love to talk about their medical histories."

"Or lack thereof with my abuela. I honestly don't understand how she's lived so long. She hates going to the doctor."

"She's one tough abuela."

"She's stubborn. I say we stay in here until Shawn is ready to go for sure. We need the wind in everyone's face and blocking some of their conversations."

"I'm sorry if you were embarrassed, I thought it was fun."

Fun?

"Your idea of fun is interesting."

"You have so much to be grateful for."

"I know."

My family regularly embarrassed me, but they were here for me in ways Lily's family wouldn't ever be for her.

"I'm outta here!" Tío Pedro called out from the boat. He lept off the back and swam toward us.

"They must be still talking about mammograms," Lily said. Then she pointed to a gray fin in the water cruising closer to us. "Hey, look!"

"Shark!" Mom stood and screamed with her hands cupping her mouth.

"It's one of the dolphins!" Lily called back.

Pedro swam to join us treading water. The dolphin began circling us.

"This is amazing." Lily was beaming. "If only my camera were waterproof."

"Pedro!" Tía Carmen shouted. "Don't touch it!"

"I don't understand why she's so convinced I would touch it," Pedro told us. He yelled back to Tía Carmen, "I told you, I have never harassed a wild animal in my entire life! I've never even gone hunting."

"I think we're technically swimming with a dolphin after all," I said. It didn't stick around long with the shouting to and from the boat but zipped back to follow the rest of the pod out to deeper water. We weren't far from the little island, so I suggested we swim in that direction. The water became gradually more shallow and before I stopped swimming, Lily began walking beside me.

Tío Pedro opted to stay and float in the water. I stood up and took Lily's hand and then we ran to the shore. The sand on the island was nearly white, and tall seagrasses covered the land where it ended. Beyond the two boats, no other land was in sight, only the blue-gray ocean. Others were still in the water, but so far we were alone on this tiny island.

I followed Lily, wading in the small waves lapping against the beach. The sun was warm on my bare back, and the view was incredible. But nothing more so than the beautiful woman beside me.

"Seeing dolphins in the wild is so much cooler than seeing them in the aquarium."

"I agree." I gestured to my Tío Pedro floating with his ample belly in the air. "But my Mexican uncle floating by is sure to keep them away."

"You think the dolphin understood what Carmen said about him being a dolphin harasser?"

"Maybe," I said with a chuckle.

"My sister would be the one scaring away the dolphins." She paused and eyed me thoughtfully. "Have Pedro and Carmen always been like this?"

I considered for a moment, then nodded. "For as long as I can remember. They always argue about silly things. I wish they'd talk more. My parents too. My dad would spend all day out on the lake with his fishing boat if he could."

"They had quite the argument over fishing versus hula."

"It's almost anything versus fishing. I wish they would have more meaningful conversations with each other. Perhaps they could avoid some of their issues."

"It's hard for some people to share their feelings."

"I agree." The same had been so true for us. "But the result of not talking is..." I gestured toward Tío Pedro, floating in the water, ignoring Tía Carmen.

Lily twisted her lip. "Yeah, it definitely all comes out one way or another if you keep difficult feelings about something to yourself long enough."

I nodded. I really wished Lily and I had been more open with each other in the past. I only made things harder by working so much.

Lily bent down to retrieve a round shell. "Shhh!" she hissed at me as she stood, rubbing it between her fingers. "Don't tell Juanita."

I watched her pink lips, recalling how soft they were and the sensation of kissing them twice last night. I resisted the powerful urge to pull her into my arms. My heart was pounding like a basketball bouncing on a gym floor.

I couldn't do that, not knowing how she felt about me. We'd been pretending so much—I didn't know what was real anymore. I knew for sure I wanted her closer to me but didn't know at all if that was what was good for us.

"Your secret is safe with me," I said. "Always."

Chapter Fourteen

Lily

When he said he'd keep my secret, my knees weakened and I wanted to grab onto his arm for support. But if I did that, he might get the wrong impression that I wanted to be closer to him. Physically. Emotionally. All of it.

Except it wouldn't be the wrong impression. I did want him closer. Close like last evening when my lips were tangled up with his. I couldn't turn away from his beautiful eyes as my blood charged through my heart like a cavalry.

He looked away first, back toward the boats.

"We should probably get back before Shawn has to yell for us."

"You think they're done talking about uncomfortable topics for you?"

"Nope. They're never done with that." His eyes sharpened. "What do you mean 'for me'?"

"I can handle it. But can you?"

"Of course. I only suggested we go swimming because you wanted to so much."

"Okay. I'll pretend to believe that." I waded into the water and Joel followed right behind.

"You're so good at pretending, by the way," he said.

If he only knew how much I wasn't pretending when he kissed me after our dance.

"Thank you. Do you think I have a future in acting?"

"I'm sure I don't."

"I don't know. I think you make a convincing enough husband." I batted my eyes at him and he wagged his eyebrows up and down.

"Do I?"

We were waist-deep in the water and he reached out, grasped my hand, and pulled me toward him. I landed against his firm chest. I couldn't breathe. My nose was maybe an inch from his chin. His lips were mesmerizing. My brain was as wobbly as my legs in the moving water.

His family was at a distance but could still see us from the boats. This was all for show, wasn't it? But the look in his eyes seemed so sincere, so tender.

I never wanted to be kissed so much in my entire life. My lips drifted slightly closer to his...

"Come on, you lovebirds!" Tía Juanita shouted.

We stepped apart and I threw myself forward in the water, swimming as fast as I could back to the boat. The exercise helped me come back to my senses. Convincing myself Joel wanted me was a risky gamble.

Either he did have a future in acting...or he was starting to want me as much as I wanted him. But why would he want me now when he hadn't before?

Once everyone was back on the boats, we cruised around seeing more dolphins in the distance and even sea lions. Flocks of seagulls sailed through the air above us as we whizzed across the water. Joel kept his arm around my shoulders and I nestled against his soft bare chest. It was warm and tantalizing. My pulse was erratic, and I didn't have any idea what his parents were trying to shout to me over the sound of the motor. My senses were going wild. I'd thrown my sundress back on but Joel had merely wrapped a towel around his shorts.

His breath tickled my ear as he whispered, "They're asking if you want to go shopping later. They need to get a few more things for the luau."

I forced myself to look him in the eye and not think about his lips, then I turned to his parents. "I'd love to go!"

Hopefully, once we were away from all the eyes around us, and Joel didn't need to have his arm around me like this (oh, the bliss mixed with torture), my brain would snap back and be able to think clearly.

Once we made it back to the dock, Joel moved away from me and slipped his shirt back on.

Carmen came up to me once we were off the boat and pinched my shoulder. "I love watching the two of you. I can tell how much Joel loves you. It's so sweet."

"Oh...thanks..." Was that the right thing to say? We were fooling them. My stomach twisted like a corkscrew.

Another side of me wondered if what she was saying was true.

Joel was talking to Juanita and his mother. He smiled when he saw me watching him. A whirlwind of guilt mixed with hope was swirling inside me.

Joel and I went shopping that evening with his parents, gathering everything from the party store that was even remotely related to a Hawaiian luau.

Abuela's children had put their money together to hire a caterer for the event who would bring folding tables and chairs. Eva found long grass table skirts, silk flower garlands, and leis. There was also a lively debate about whether or not to buy inflatable palm trees. Armando thought they would only blow away in the wind. Joel thought they were tacky, but Eva thought they were cute. I reminded them all there were a few real palm trees between the resort and the beach, so they decided that would do.

"Have you decided which song you're going to sing?" Eva asked me once we loaded the trunk of the car with all they'd bought. Some of the bags had to go in the back seat with us. Joel packed them in the seat to the far right.

I paused. After asking Abuela what she wanted me to sing, she'd told me to decide on my own.

"There's a cool rap version of *Endless Love* I'm psyched about." I winked at Joel and he clamped his lips closed, trying not to laugh.

Eva blinked at me and stared.

"I'm kidding."

She visibly breathed out. "Oh, how funny you are."

Joel opened the door to the back of the car for me, and I slipped into the seat and slid over to the middle seat, against the shopping bags. He sat beside me and we were squished as closely as possible in the small back seat of his parents' compact car.

His sweet and spicy scent and the firm warmth against my shoulder threatened to melt my skin.

"Do you have enough room?" He asked, trying to shift more toward the door but not moving much at all.

"I'm fine," I whispered. I truly was. I was safe beside him.

"Perhaps you could sing something from *Evita*. It's Mamá's favorite musical," Eva suggested from the passenger seat.

"I thought her favorite was *Cats*," Armando said, turning around to back out of the parking space.

"Don't be ridiculous," Eva said. "She's always had dogs, never cats. Why would she like a musical where they sing?"

"Plenty of people like *Cats* who don't have cats," Armando insisted.

"Oh, really?"

Armando sighed. "I'm sure whatever Lily wants to sing will be lovely."

"You are right about that," Joel said with his eyes on me.

"Perhaps I should see if there's a traditional song that goes with luaus."

"Just don't ask Phoenix the hippie for help with linguistics."

"That Phoenix fellow seemed very good with Hawaiian to me," Armando said.

Armando must have never heard the language spoken before.

Joel scoffed, "If by that you mean clueless, then sure."

"I liked it," Eva said with a short, firm nod. "It was the hula dance I didn't care for. Too sensual and inappropriate for someone Mamá's age."

"Abuela seemed to have fun. She didn't go too far, I hope. Lily was quite good at it." Joel nudged me, and I knew my cheeks were turning red.

"You could use some more practice, I think."

"I'll be happy to if you practice with me."

He locked eyes with me in the dim light and a smile spread across my face. "I'd be happy to."

Chapter Fifteen
Lily

That evening there were no group plans and everyone scattered to find dinner. I convinced Joel to take my cousin's offer to use the tickets to the French restaurant. I hadn't tried it. I didn't exactly know what would be on the menu, but I was up for an adventure.

"Are you sure?" he asked as we stepped up to the entrance, almost obscured with indoor plants and potted shrubs.

"It's free food," I said with a shrug. I say we give it a try."

"Welcome to Le Rivage," said a man with a thick brown mustache. He wore a black suit and I wondered if my floral summer dress was appropriate for this place. Joel wore a navy jacket and had perfectly ironed pants and shiny shoes.

"How many?" the host asked.

"Table for two," Joel said.

He took two menus from the shelf below the podium, then said, "Follow me, please."

Joel offered me his arm and I accepted. None of his family was here. It was only us. Was he simply being a gentleman or did he want me closer?

We weaved around the unnecessary amount of plants. In the dining room, there was a wall of floor-to-ceiling windows to our left. The sun was down, but during the daylight, it would likely have a great view, if not for the plants and potted trees all along it. Someone seated at the tables near the window would likely only have a good view of the leaves. The lighting was so dim, with only a few small candles on each round table. The tables weren't very big—only large enough for two chairs—and were covered in white tablecloths.

"Someone really likes plants up here," I said. The host showed us to a table right next to the biggest fern I had ever seen.

Joel sat down across from me and studied the plant. "It's strange they wouldn't want us to see the ocean. When the sun is up, the view from this window is sure to be incredible."

"Here is our wine list," the host said as he patted a card on the end of the table closest to him. "I'll give you a few moments." Then he spun on his heel and walked away.

"Did we offend him?" Joel asked. "I saw him roll his eyes before he left."

I shrugged. "I hope not."

I surveyed the empty room. It wasn't very late, and this should be a prime dinner hour. "It's not a great sign to be alone in the dining room."

Joel nodded. "The food might be terrible."

"I'll have words with Chris if he gave us free passes for a bad restaurant." My cousin did love pranks. I just didn't think he'd pull one when he met my ex/fake husband.

Joel suggested a wine off the list and I agreed. But no one came to take our drink order.

"Are there any other employees here?" Joel asked.

"This may be a bad time to mention...my cousin might be trying to get me back for the glitter bombs I planted in his office."

Joel raised an eyebrow. "You? A glitter bomb?"

"Yeah, not my best prank, but I filled cups with glitter and tied them with a string to the cabinets in his office. It took longer than I thought for him to need to open one of the doors, but when he did, glitter poured everywhere." I clamped my hand over my mouth, stopping a laugh. "It's impossible to vacuum it all up," I mumbled through my fingers.

Joel's eyes sparkled with amusement. "And *why* did you do this?"

I sighed. "Okay, it started in high school. He used to fill my car up with balloons on my birthday, and I covered his car with silly string and stuck Oreo halves to the sides."

"There are so many things I never knew about you, Lily."

I placed my hands on the table and batted my eyes overdramatically. "Would you like to know more?"

"Absolutely."

Before I could answer, I saw a sight that, perhaps, I should have expected.

"Phoenix," I said, as he waltzed over in a solid black collar shirt. He had a tie-dyed apron tied around his dark jeans.

"How's it going over here?"

Joel clamped his hand around his mouth again, face muscles straining, trying not to laugh.

"May I suggest our newest wine, Chateau Mouton Rothschild?" Phoenix's French pronunciation sounded authentic to me. Not that I spoke any French. I hoped my eyes weren't bugging out. His work massacring the Hawaiian mele gave me no clue he knew any other language.

"Yes, please," I answered. Joel was still struggling across from me, but Phoenix didn't seem to notice. "We were discussing that one."

"Got it." He pulled a small notepad from his apron pocket and wrote it down. "Tonight, the special is salmon en papillote. But, I recommend the lamb shank navarin."

"I'll have the salmon." I could not believe this guy. Did he seriously speak French? He was filled with surprises. He was also everywhere around here. What other jobs did he have?

Joel hadn't recovered. Both hands were clamped over his mouth now.

"Would you like the salmon too?" I asked him.

He nodded, eyes straining.

"Are you okay, man?" Phoenix finally looked away from me to see Joel's face. "Lemme get you some water."

He then dashed back to the kitchen.

"Pull yourself together. He thinks you're dying."

Joel dropped his hands and let himself laugh out loud. He leaned his head on one hand, placing his elbow on the table. "That guy is every freaking where."

"So it seems. He's a man of many talents." I pointed toward the kitchen. "Do you think you can get yourself together before he comes back?"

"I'll try." He settled down his laughter and wiped tears from his eyes. "As long as he doesn't try to hug us, it should be fine."

Phoenix came back with water for both of us and two glasses of wine. The salmon was terrible, and I started sneezing, probably from the proximity of all these plants. But my companion for the evening was perfect.

———ell———

We went back to the room after dinner and snacked on microwave popcorn while we watched a movie. The pillow wall was still in the center of the bed, and we sat on either side of it. Both of us were on the edges, as far away from each other as possible.

Joel's aunts were arguing in the hallway. It was loud, but since it was all in Spanish I didn't know what they were saying.

"What's going on out there?"

Joel's face twisted as he held a handful of popcorn near his mouth. "It sounds like they're fighting about the catering arrangements for the luau. But it's pretty spicy language."

"Stop acting like I can't handle adult language."

"I'm just embarrassed."

I could sympathize. I was rather embarrassed by my sister's behavior at the reunion.

Joel's mother joined in out in the hallway and things got even louder for a while. When it finally died down, it was quiet for some time, and the movie we were watching ended. It was time to sneak out.

Joel followed me to the door and I opened it slowly as he hovered behind me.

The hall was empty and silent.

"I'm going to go for it," I whispered, turning back to him. "Good night."

"Good night."

I slipped off my flip-flops and tiptoed down the hall barefoot. I didn't get far before a door swung open and Rosa stepped out.

"Hey, Lily. What's up?"

I froze, my muscles stiff. "Hey."

"Where're ya heading?"

"Oh, I, uh..." I tried to paste on a smile, but I was afraid I probably looked like I was guilty of something.

"She was going to get some ice," Joel offered from the doorway.

"Oh, cool," She said, grinning. "I'll walk with you and get some too. Let me grab my ice bucket. Where's yours?"

"Oops," I said. Ice bucket. I needed one. "Almost forgot."

"At least you didn't get far," Rosa said, then ducked back into her room.

I backed up to Joel's door and he handed me the ice bucket. I dropped my flip-flops to the floor and slipped back in them.

"Sorry," he whispered.

I snatched it from him as Rosa popped out into the hall again.

"Ready." Her smile was so chipper, I knew I couldn't fake it that far. But at least she wasn't asking any more questions about me creeping through the hallway.

I forced my lips to curl and hoped it didn't look freaky. My nerves were still on alert from being caught. I needed to relax and not give her any reason to be suspicious.

We walked down the hall toward the elevator. The ice machine was to the right in an alcove, along with two vending machines.

"Did you need a break from Joel?" Rosa asked with a wink, as she put her bucket under the spout that released the ice.

"Ha," I said. Should I say yes? Would she laugh, or would that lead to gossip that we were having problems?

We're not having problems anymore. We're divorced.

"I'm only joking." She nudged me with her elbow. "You should see your face."

Crap. What does my face look like?

"You're not *really* having troubles are you?" Her eyes were filled with concern as the ice dropped into the bucket.

I knew it. I look like I'm hiding a huge secret.

"No," I said, waving it away with a large swoop of my right hand. "Everything is *fine*."

Why does my voice sound so high?

"We're having a great time." I put my bucket in position and pushed the button. "I just...I like a lot of ice. I'm a *huge* fan of ice. I always run out. Joel was getting tired of coming out here, and I thought it was my turn."

She stared at me for a few heartbeats. I could hear mine banging like a conga drum.

She thinks I'm crazy.

"Oh, you know what?" She tapped my arm. "It's funny. You should see my dad."

"Mateo likes lots of ice?"

She nodded and leaned the bucket against her side with one arm, then flicked her other hand to the side. "There's barely any soda in his glass for all the ice."

"That's me exactly." I forced a laugh. *Yack.* Now I needed to remember to pack my drinks with ice.

"You fit right in this crazy family."

There it is. She thinks I'm crazy, but that works for the Sanchez crowd.

We walked back slowly to our rooms while Rosa asked me more questions about my life as a teacher. I answered them on autopilot, my nerves still a wreck, as we got closer to her door. I thought we'd stop there, but she kept going toward Joel's room. He'd left the door ajar for me.

"I'm looking forward to hearing you perform," Rosa said, then nudged my shoulder with hers. "Don't let Joel drive you too crazy, now."

"Oh, I won't," I said in a high-pitched voice, pushing the door open with my foot.

Joel was sitting on the bed and when I came in he jumped to his feet. I shoved the ice bucket at him as the heavy door swung closed with a loud thud.

"I made a fool of myself." I breathed in and out slowly. "If anyone asks, I'm obsessed with ice."

"Okay..." His lips twisted. "I'm sorry about that."

I didn't know how I'd be able to try sneaking out again. My stomach tied itself into a pretzel as I thought about it.

"Here, why don't you just stay tonight?" He set the ice down on the desk. "You can have the bed."

He took a pillow from the wall we'd made and tossed it on the couch.

"The couch is too small for you." It was closer to the size of a loveseat. "The pillow wall should be good enough, right?"

Was I kidding myself here? He shifted from one foot to the other, "Um, yeah. We did it once, right?"

"Yep."

I repeated it to myself over and over. I took a pair of leggings and a T-shirt from my suitcase and went to the bathroom to change.

We'd done this before. We'd been in the same bed and nothing had happened. Of course it had been an accident, but still...why were those kisses we shared at the reunion replaying in my mind with the intensity of a firework finale?

I did not want to fall for Joel again. That fireworks show we once had together only fizzed out. I took a deep breath. We were friends now, right?

Friends.

That's what I needed to think of him as. I'd eaten plenty of popcorn in the same bed with my friends at sleepovers. But no friend of mine was ever a hot guy who dipped me on the dance floor like Joel had. When I closed my eyes, I thought I could still feel his lips on mine.

I splashed cold water on my face to snap out of it.

When I came out of the bathroom, I walked over to the left side of the bed where I'd been eating popcorn not too long before. My leggings were full length and my T-shirt was pretty baggy.

Joel took his pajamas to the bathroom and stayed for a while. I sat down on the edge of the bed and picked up stray popcorn pieces.

Once he came out, he was wearing long sleeves and loose gray pants with matching socks. He had on plenty of clothes. I was overthinking this.

"I'll sleep on top of the comforter again," I offered, going for the blanket in the closet.

"I don't mind doing that." Joel was standing by the other side of the bed.

I was too nervous to argue, so I tossed the blanket to him. "Okay."

I pulled the covers back in a corner, trying not to disturb the pillow wall, and slipped into bed, facing the wall.

The mattress shifted as Joel lay down on his side and spread the blanket out over him.

"Good night," he murmured and turned off the lamp on the table beside him.

I moaned as I pretended to yawn and reached out to switch off the lamp by me.

"Good night."

I tried not to think about our kiss anymore. Or how close he was to me in the dark.

Everything is fine.

Chapter Sixteen

Joel

Seagulls outside called out in loud "ha-ha-ha" sounds and light escaped from the top of the closed curtain covering the balcony doors. I barely registered the warm pressure against my body and struggled to open my eyes. Was the pillow wall on top of me?

My hand moved and brushed over bare skin. My eyes shot open and I saw Lily snuggled up against me, her arm lying over my chest.

My heart took off like a dog after a squirrel. She was beautiful curled up against me. Her hair spread out across my pillow, and I so badly wanted to reach out and comb my fingers through it. I was afraid to wake her up. I carefully lifted my head and saw the pillow wall was scattered across the large bed.

How could I forget how much she sometimes rolled around in her sleep?

It hadn't been easy to fall asleep, knowing she was in my bed with pillows blocking us. If she'd made it this far before I'd fallen asleep, I never would have closed my eyes.

I laid my head back down and waited for her to wake up. This was dangerous. She was warm and soft and put all my senses on alert. I wanted to bend down and kiss her forehead.

Then her lips.

I tried to think of things that turned me off the most: doing my taxes, that reality show about hoarders, and that time my parents gave me the sex talk.

Lily stirred in my arms and yawned as she opened her eyes. "Joel?"

It took her a few more seconds to register where she was.

Lily's head popped up, her eyebrows reaching for her hairline. Her lips were inches from mine, and once she glanced at them she pushed on my chest, thrusting herself away from me.

"What happened to the pillow wall?" She smoothed her hair out of her face as she sat up and looked around at the bed.

"It didn't make it." I pushed up on one elbow and couldn't help smiling.

She jumped out of bed like a rabbit standing on a hot plate.

"Lily, are you okay?" I called as she rushed to the bathroom.

Perhaps she needed some space. I sure did.

I got out of bed and went to the balcony. Cool wind in my face might help.

The red and orange lights of the sunrise brushed across the sky to begin the day. The water slapped the sandy beach in a steady rhythm. Only a few people were out this early, walking down the beach. Brown pelicans cruised by in a row nearly at eye level, and I wished I'd grabbed my phone before I came out. It would make a stunning photo.

I breathed in the fresh, salty air, wishing my life were less complicated—and berating myself for making it this way.

Lily and I hadn't left things in a good place at all a year ago. Yet, she'd leaped into action when we thought Abuela was dying. I didn't deserve her.

I don't know how long I was out there, but I woke up in the chair on the balcony to Lily singing, "Good morning!"

I sat up and rubbed my eyes with my thumb and forefinger. "Good morning."

She sat down in the chair a few feet away and crossed her legs. Her feet were bare and showed off her sparkly magenta toenails.

She'd piled her hair on her head in a messy bun. I loved the way she looked with no makeup on.

"Sorry, I wasn't trying to be obnoxious," she said.

"No, it's fine. I didn't realize I fell asleep."

She was smiling but I saw anxiety in her eyes. She held onto her knee a little too tightly.

"I'm, uh, sorry about..." She tilted her head toward the bed. "That."

"Don't be. I hope you were having sweet dreams."

Her cheeks colored and she looked away.

Had she been dreaming about me?

"You're an early bird still." Her voice was wobbly. I didn't want to make her more uncomfortable so I went with the subject change.

"I love those early worms."

"I know." She nodded and folded her arms tightly. "You love worms."

What could we do to kill the awkwardness?

"You aren't going to sing the song?" I asked.

"What?" Her lip twisted and she lifted one eyebrow. "The camp song about big, fat, juicy ones?"

I nodded.

She grinned. "How about I sing that for Abuela?"

"Please do. I'll have my phone ready to record it for YouTube."

"Perfect," she said with a giggle.

"What are you going to sing for her?"

"It's a surprise." She pressed her lips together and pretended to zip them.

"You're not going to even tell me?"

"Nope." She shook her head.

"Well, whatever it is, even the worm song, I'm sure it will be great."

"You have so much confidence in me." Her voice was quiet.

"I've seen you perform."

"I..." she glanced down at her toes, then back up at me. "I want you to know it means a lot to me."

"I've always believed in you."

Our eyes met and my heart skipped. I wanted to take her in my arms and hold her like a life raft.

I was falling for her again. An icy sensation crept over me an instant later. This time I knew for sure it would end. There wasn't a trial period and a time for us to decide what to do. There was an end date to our charade.

I gripped the arms of the plastic chair and pushed myself to my feet. "Would you like some coffee?"

"Well," she uttered.

I pulled open the sliding glass door and hurried inside. I was a coward.

Someone knocked on the door, and when I went to look through the peephole, I saw Rosa standing there in peach pajamas.

"Joel, it's time. Hurry."

I opened the door. "I almost forgot. Let me grab Lily."

Other family members were spilling out from their rooms into the hall.

Lily walked inside and slid the door I'd left open to a close. "What's up?"

"It's a tradition to wake Abuela up with a birthday song," Rosa explained. "We sing Las Mañanitas."

"Oh, how sweet. Is she still asleep?"

Rosa nodded. "We believe so."

"Let me get dressed..." Lily glanced down and slid her hands from her baggy shirt to her leggings.

"No, we go like this." Rosa patted the legs of her pajamas.

"Okay."

"Let's go." I took Lily's hand and we went with Rosa as the family gathered around in the hall outside Abuela's room. I pulled my phone from my pocket and called up the lyrics, then gave it to Lily.

Dad raised a hand and said, "On three. One, two, three."

We sang, and Lily did her best to pronounce the words and follow along. Soon, the door opened and Abuela stuck her head out. I didn't know she could smile so widely.

When we finished, she had tears in her eyes. "Gracias! Gracias!" She laid a hand over her heart. "I'm so grateful for all of you."

"It is us," I said, "who are grateful for you."

She pulled me close and kissed my forehead. "Now what's for breakfast?"

"Anything you want," I said.

"Good, I plan to eat my weight in sausage."

My mom's eyes went wide, but she said nothing.

"As I said, Abuela," I placed my arm around her shoulders. "Anything you want."

That afternoon the caterers arrived with the tables and chairs and Lily and I helped set up. We carried the bags from my parents' car and worked on hanging the grass table skirts. Tía Carmen stacked hula hoops on the sand beside the head table.

"I thought it would be fun to have a contest," she said as I clipped a flower garland to another table nearby.

"I love that idea," Lily said, taking a hula hoop and stepping into it. She spun it around and moved her hips to keep it going in circles.

It was a hypnotizing sight and I couldn't look away. I was weak. I couldn't believe I'd awoken with her in my arms.

She laughed at me and shot me a look with a challenge in her eye.

"Grab a hoop, Velásquez."

I obeyed and did my best to keep it from falling to my feet. Once we got a good rhythm going, Tía Juanita came to stand in front of us and watched us with her hands on her petite hips. "It's not time for the contest yet, you two."

"Joel needs practice." Lily winked at me and I lost momentum. The hoop whirled down to the sand.

"Yes, I see." Tía Juanita nodded, then stepped over to pat Joel on the shoulder. "Good try."

"I was doing pretty good until Lily distracted me."

"Ha!" Lily's hoop was still bouncing in circles around her hips. There was a fluttering in my chest and the air around me was so warm. "Blaming me is all too convenient, bruh."

Everything about her made everything seem better.

"Have I mentioned that I'm the reigning hula hoop champion at Walhalla Summer Camp?"

"I surrender." I stepped out of the hoop and picked it up.

Rosa hurried over with her phone to take a video of Lily. Her hoop was still going strong.

"You're killing it," Rosa said, holding her phone with one hand and giving her a thumbs up with the other.

My cousin Lulu's seven-year-old twins, Maddie and Gabriella, were playing tag. Maddie zipped around the tables being set up and straight for Lily, Gabriella following close behind.

I tried to catch Maddie before she dived, but she leaped right between Lily's legs. Lily dropped her hoop and then fell backward. As I grabbed her, Gabriella tripped on the hoop and fell into the sand.

I held Lily in my arms, enjoying it far too much, as Tía Juanita yelled at the girls with a long Spanish lecture.

"It's okay, no one is hurt," Lily insisted, pushing away from me."

Tía Juanita shook her head. "I told you, it is bad luck to run between someone's legs. Maddie needs to go back through the other direction or she'll never grow up to her full height."

Lily blinked and looked at me. I shrugged. Most of us had decided a long time ago it was pointless to tell Tía Juanita it was nonsense.

I crouched down and pulled the stunned girls into a hug.

Rosa rolled her eyes and sighed. "Tía Juanita..."

"Should she go through the hula hoop as well?" Lily picked up the hoop, face uncertain.

"That won't be necessary, I'm sure," Tía Juanita said.

"Okay." Lily tossed her hula hoop to the side, then spread her legs and planted her hands on her hips like Wonder Woman.

"Now, Maddie, go ahead, but this way." Tía Juanita pointed to the ocean.

Rosa sighed. Maddie nodded and I let her go.

Maddie didn't need to bend down to walk through.

"Can I?" Gabriella asked, rubbing a tear away from her face.

Lily smiled and waved her over. "Sure! Come right through."

The girls went around in circles under her legs several times, giggling along the way. Lily started singing *Wheels on the Bus*, and the girls joined in as they kept going around and around.

It was so adorable—I thought my heart would pop.

Tía Juanita was satisfied. She smiled, then turned to go back to work helping set up.

"Okay, that's enough of that." My cousin Lulu, the girls' mother, marched over and snatched the giggling girls one by one away from Lily.

"I'm sorry about all this."

Lily shook her head quickly. "Oh no, we were having a good time."

"You are so patient. Joel, you be good to this woman." Lulu turned to me. "Kim was never good with kids. I'm not superstitious, but even I think that's bad luck."

"I second that," Rosa chimed in.

Lily shifted from one foot to the other. She opened her mouth but said nothing.

"She's a music teacher," I said, taking the excuse to walk over and squeeze her shoulder. "She's used to kids."

"High school kids though..." Lily rubbed her elbows and refused to meet anyone's eyes.

Lulu waved her free hand dismissively, holding Maddie with one arm. "It's still a good sign that you haven't run screaming from this loud and crazy family. I can see why Joel married you. He still can't take his eyes off you after a whole year." She walked around Lily to poke me as she was leaving. "It's adorable, cuz."

Lily's cheeks colored and she gazed toward the ocean, not looking my way.

Chapter Seventeen

Joel

I helped Tío Mateo set up Tiki torches in the sand around the party zone. As we worked, twisting them down into the sand, the sun sank low in the sky. It would be setting soon and the area would have a soft glow. Rosa passed out leis, and everyone was dressed in either Hawaiian shirts or floral dresses in bright colors.

Lily had disappeared, and when I'd gone up to my room to change, she wasn't there. My heart was heavy as I changed into the shirt my mom insisted I wear. It was filled with orange flowers loud enough to make anyone close to me go deaf.

I tried Lily's phone but she didn't answer. I sat on the bed, strength draining from my body. I didn't want to see her go.

I loved her silly expressions when she tried to make me laugh, and the passionate look in her eyes as her fingers danced across the piano keys. I wished she knew how wonderful a person she was. She made my knees turn to jelly and my heart do cartwheels.

I wanted to be near her all the time and it was scaring the hell out of me.

I wasn't falling—I was gone.

I went back downstairs and back out to the beach.

The scent of pineapple and roasted pork wafted in the breeze. Shades of red and orange streaked across the sky. Tío Mateo was acting as the DJ with a sound system set up at the far end of the party.

The circular tables were decorated with flower-filled pineapples as centerpieces. The caterers had set up two long buffet tables which were now filled with large fruit trays and platters of rolls and pulled pork.

A cake made to look like a pineapple was on another table, surrounded by cupcakes topped with tall swirls of yellow frosting. The steady beat of the waves hitting the shore was soothing...until Tío Mateo decided to play *Pump Up the Jam*.

Tía Carmen made a slicing motion with her hand across her neck. She wore a turquoise dress with a purple flower pattern.

"What's the problem?" Tío Mateo frowned, spreading his hands out. "You told me to choose the music."

"Mamá likes Elvis," Tía Carmen called to him with her hands cupping her mouth. "Play *Can't Help Falling in Love*."

Tío Mateo grumbled but cut the music and tapped around on the laptop connected to the sound system. "Fine, but next I'm playing the *Macarena*."

"Don't you dare," Tía Carmen warned, trying to use her expression to attempt to slice him in two.

As Elvis's voice sang out, I glanced around, still not seeing Lily. She still wasn't answering her phone.

Ice crept up my spine.

Was she too nervous about her solo? Would she really leave now? Like this?

Without saying goodbye, again?

Abuela was seated at a table with her daughters, being waited on hand and foot. My family members were filling their plates and taking their food to the tables.

I wasn't hungry. I sank into an empty chair at an empty table. Where was my fake wife? How long until someone would ask? This was crazy. I was a mess.

It was time to come clean. But first, this was Abuela's birthday.

I dragged myself up and made myself smile. I hugged my abuela, kissed her cheek, and with full sincerity, "¡Feliz cumpleaños!"

"Gracias, querido." She gripped my chin and kissed both of my cheeks. "Everything is so beautiful. I love it." She glanced around. "Where is your sweet wife?"

"She's..." My heart raced. "There's something I need to tell you..."

"I'm sorry I'm a little late." Lily came up behind me, placing a hand on my shoulder. I wanted to stand up but my knees wouldn't work.

"Happy birthday, Josephina."

"Gracias, Lily." Abuela's eyes sparkled with delight. "That dress is lovely."

She was wearing a long, white dress with red tropical flowers that wrapped around one shoulder and left the other bare. It complimented her curves in all the right ways.

Her hair was twisted up behind her and clipped with a big silk flower.

Abuela then patted the peach-colored fabric of her dress. "I wish I looked half as good in this."

"You look amazing," Lily assured her.

"Don't you mean I look one hundred?"

"Not a day over seventy." Lily smiled and Abuela giggled.

Abuela turned to me, "What was it you wanted to tell me?"

"Oh," I glanced at Lily and then back to Abuela. "I want to tell you how much I love you. I want you to have the best birthday ever."

"Oh, darling. I'm already having the best day of my life." She gave me a little shove. "Now, get up and ask your wife to dance."

Lily offered me her hand. I took it and sparks shot through my hand and up my arm. I found the strength to stand and we walked over to the patch of open sand in between the tables and Tío Mateo's equipment station.

"Where were you? I tried calling several times."

"I had to go back to my apartment for this dress. I'm sorry. I didn't plug my phone in last night and it died."

My muscles relaxed, and she narrowed her eyes. "Are you okay? I'm sorry if I worried you."

"I'm fine." Everything was fine now. She was here. I don't think I've ever found an Elvis song so sexy before. I held Lily in my arms and we slow danced.

I held her close, and she leaned her soft face against mine. I couldn't have dreamed of a woman more beautiful.

"Does this remind you of anything?" she whispered.

I was in a trance. The words barely made sense to me. "What?"

"Elvis."

"Oh!" I cracked up and held her tighter. "Of course, our *perfect* wedding." I backed away just enough to meet her eyes. "This wasn't the song he sang, was it?"

"No, I believe it was *Love Me Tender*."

I shook my head. "Honestly, I wasn't paying all that much attention to the guy. The only one I saw was you."

She held my gaze and I leaned my nose against hers. My body was aching to kiss her, but Tía Carmen tapped me on the shoulder.

"I'll announce Lily in five minutes."

"I'll be ready," Lily said, dropping my hand.

"Are you still not going to tell me what song you chose?"

"You'll see." She smiled with her lips pressed together.

A few minutes later, Tía Carmen took a microphone from Tío Mateo and a loud feedback loop squealed, making everyone wince.

"I want to thank everyone for coming. I know we all want to wish our mamá and abuela a very happy birthday."

The family cheered and shouted "¡Feliz cumpleaños!"

"Joel's wife, Lily, has offered to sing for Mamá. Here she is," Lily stepped over to Tía Carmen, took the microphone, then nodded to Tío Mateo. He turned on the music with a piano playing soft, slow jazz.

Abuela's face lit up like a neon sign and she clasped her hands together over her chest. "I love Ella!" she cried.

Lily sang Ella Fitzgerald's *Misty.* Her voice was smooth and sultry. The song was about a woman whose eyes misted over when she was holding her lover's hand and when they were together.

Cheesy, yes, but it didn't sound that way when she sang it. It was bewitching. Once she reached the last line, she sang the word "you" and looked directly at me.

I tugged at the collar of my shirt. Why was it so hot out here when the sun was setting? My brain was scrambled like the eggs I'd had for breakfast.

Chapter Eighteen
Lily

I loved Ella Fitzgerald, and I took a wild guess that Josephina would like this song. I happily watched the joy spread over her face. She was adorable with her loving brown eyes and white hair up in yellow flower clips.

I couldn't help it. My eyes drifted to Joel as I sang. I had been close to misty-eyed when he'd said that thing about only seeing me at our wedding.

I thought I'd lost my mind when I let that man wreck my plans to be single.

It was so last minute. I'd questioned myself every day of our time together if love could really happen that fast.

If it had, we'd lost it. Was there any chance for us now?

I thought about waking up in his arms and the glorious few seconds it was before I was awake enough to remember how that wasn't supposed to happen.

I finished up my song and then went back to my seat next to Joel while the family applauded.

Joel kissed me on the cheek when I sat down, leaving my face warm and tingly. I didn't want this to end, feeling like I was part of his big, loud, crazy, loving family. But mostly, I didn't want to end this pretend world where I belonged with Joel. Everyone would be leaving tomorrow afternoon, and I'd go back to my apartment and the single life I didn't want anymore.

Despite all our issues in the past, could we be something now? Could we conquer the hardship of long distance?

Would he want me that much?

I needed my sister's voice out of my head, telling me so many times it was my fault my relationships didn't last.

"Are you okay?" Joel whispered in my ear, knocking every thought out of my head.

"Yeah."

"Is there something on your mind?"

A thousand somethings...but when your lips are close to my ear I can't remember anything.

When I didn't answer, he said, "You were incredible. Abuela loved it. We all did."

"Thank you." I faced him, wondering if he could see the question behind my eyes as I gazed at him. *Can we try again?*

I opened my mouth, wanting to speak, but the blaring sounds of the *Macarena* blasted through the air all around us. Carmen hopped up from her table and marched over to scold her brother, but not before at least half of the family was out of their seats and dancing.

This snapped me out of it and I seized Joel's hand and pulled him back over to the patch of sand AKA the dance floor.

"Are you serious? This is *not* dancing," he protested.

I made the motions with my hands along with the beat. He needed a little coaxing. "Dare you."

I slapped the sides of my hips and rocked along with everyone else, then turned around.

I glanced at him over my shoulder and saw him grin.

"Challenge accepted." Joel then thrust out his hands one at a time and did the Macarena.

I would never get tired of watching this man dance. Even if it was the Macarena.

We taste-tested the cupcakes and decided to give them a 9.5. The cake was pineapple-flavored and topped with a buttercream frosting. I didn't hold back licking my fingers after I finished mine.

Joel liked the cake more than the frosting, and I said I would have liked a pile of frosting on the side. We were stuffed by the time we got back to the room.

We finished our puzzle while our stomachs settled down. I knew I'd need to move out of the hotel room tomorrow, so I brought in the towel I left to dry on the balcony and tossed it on the bed.

Joel picked it up and folded it.

My stomach twisted, remembering how annoyed he'd been with my mess when we'd lived together. He'd even put my books in rainbow-color order. I admit it looked nice, but some of the series weren't together and books by the same author were on different shelves. It was madness.

"Joel, let me get my stuff out of your way." I snatched away the towel and tossed it in my suitcase along with the other clothes I'd pulled out earlier when deciding what to wear to lunch.

"I'm sorry," he said stepping back.

"I'm sorry this is stressful for you."

"What are you talking about? This isn't stressing me."

I gestured to my suitcase. "Sharing a room with me is driving you crazy."

"No, it's not. Hey, I'm sorry if I overstepped." He held his hands up.

"You were like this when we were married." I threw my hands up, turned away from him, and tossed my makeup into a smaller bag. "You thought I was a slob. You're trying to say I don't bother you all of a sudden?"

"I never said you were a slob." His jaw went tight.

"You constantly cleaned up after me." I spun around to face him and folded my arms. "I always mean to clean up, but I get distracted and...There were all kinds of things I had no idea where you'd put when you cleaned them up."

"I wasn't stressed with you, Lily." He rubbed the bridge of his nose and sighed. "I'm neurotic about cleaning. I admit I go too far sometimes. And I did have a hard time adjusting to living with you, but–"

"You can say that again." I looked at the ceiling and sighed. This was exasperating.

"I'm sorry if you felt criticized, and I'm sorry for anything I said that hurt your feelings."

The sincerity in his eyes stopped me.

"I suppose I'm sensitive about it." That was an understatement. "I have plenty of people in my life to tell me I'm doing things wrong."

"I get it. The truth is, you were usually always busy thinking about others when I was obsessed with planning everything out and making sure everything was in order. I'm not at all surprised a normal person would find me difficult."

I met his gaze and my eyebrows slowly lifted. "You think I'm a *normal* person?"

"Not exactly."

"What then?"

"I think you're an amazing person."

I blinked, my heart missing a beat as he stepped closer.

"You're a remarkable singer, pianist, and dancer," he continued in a low voice. "I've never been to your classroom, but I have no doubt you're an awesome teacher. You're thoughtful and kind, and your smile would light the city in a blackout..." He shook his head slowly. "It makes me want to sing with my stupid swan voice."

I couldn't help giggling. His feet brought him even closer until he was inches away. "Plus, you're gorgeous."

He smoothed a hair out of my face and around my ear. My heart was thumping in my eardrums and my skin sizzled from the brief touch. As his hand dropped down, I grabbed his arm and pulled him closer. My skin was on fire, and all my nerve endings were on alert.

His eyes were on my lips and I held my breath as he moved ever closer. His lips touched mine, slowly, curiously. It was as if he were asking my permission.

I slipped my arms around his middle, and he took the encouragement and deepened the kiss. Heat from his lips shot through my body down to my toes. I didn't know if my feet were still touching the floor.

A volcano could erupt beside us at this moment and I would neither care nor notice. His hand moved down my back, and I slipped my hand under his shirt and up his spine. He broke the kiss and kissed along my jawline, then down my neck. I sighed and he recaptured my lips.

I didn't need to breathe, I just needed him closer. I nudged him backward until his legs hit the end of the bed.

He broke the kiss again and in a ragged voice, asked, "Are you sure?"

I answered with another kiss.

Chapter Nineteen

Joel

Yes, the hotel staff would clean and make the beds, but it just wasn't good enough for me. I wanted to do it my way, and I couldn't leave the room a mess when I went out for the day. My brain wouldn't let me, despite now knowing how it bothered Lily.

I was a rat. I normally knew how to clean up my messes...but I was clueless about this one. My past and present with Lily was beyond complicated. I hadn't expected the fight to end the way it did.

It was all kinds of incredible, and waking in her arms was like a dream. But as soon as she woke up, she rushed to get ready and was out the door for breakfast with my family before I even had my shirt on. It seemed like she was trying to avoid me. She barely said a word.

There was so much we hadn't figured out yet.

I hoped she'd really be downstairs.

Why was there still so much fear? I couldn't stop thinking about waking up a year ago to find out she'd left. How could I go through that again? I had to go back to Phoenix today, and the job she loved was here.

When I made it to the breakfast buffet, I found my family spread among several tables and Lily was chatting and laughing with Rosa and Lulu.

Relief washed over me. When she saw me she patted a chair she'd saved next to hers and I sat down. I tried to contribute to the conversation, but my brain was as mushy as the applesauce Gabriella was eating at the table across from us beside Lulu.

After breakfast, there was a loud round of hugging and saying goodbye. Some were leaving sooner than others throughout the day.

Everyone told me how wonderful it was to finally meet Lily. Abuela pinched both of my cheeks and hugged Lily like she was one of her granddaughters.

I hated myself.

Upstairs in the hotel room, I worked on packing the rest of my things. It was almost time to go back to our real lives and I wasn't ready. I wished we could stay longer in this pretend world.

Lily and I worked in silence to gather our things up from the room. We finally had time to talk, but how to get started eluded me. I wanted so much to know what she was thinking.

Why is this so hard?

"We can check out early and say goodbye to everyone," I said as I zipped up my suitcase. I wasn't sure what else to say. I didn't want to make her feel uncomfortable or obligated to try to make things work. That wasn't what we agreed on.

As wonderful as our time together was (and it *absolutely* was), I had a plane to catch in a few hours.

I couldn't say for sure how much of anything this week had been only pretending. Last night wasn't fake. Impulsive, maybe. But not fake. Warmth rushed through my body with the memory.

"I feel like we should talk about last night," I said, sweat beading on the back of my neck. "It was amazing...but I have to go back to Phoenix and..." I couldn't finish.

"I know it's a long way from here." Lily sat down on the bed with her small bag in her lap and fiddled with the zipper. "I'll have a break from school the week of Thanksgiving if you...well, if you'd like to try to..."

Fear rushed through me along with hope.

Unfortunately, the fear was greater.

She wanted to give long-distance a try. How many times did a situation like this work out? I was betting it was extremely rare.

"This is so complicated, Lily." I shook my head. My stomach churned and my chest tightened.

"I realize that." She sighed. "I love my job here, and I know you have to get back to work, but that doesn't mean we can't figure something out, right?"

"We've already done complicated." I rubbed the bridge of my nose and faced her. "We went too fast last time, and I don't know if we were thinking clearly this time either."

"So you feel last night was too fast?" She blinked. "What makes you think I wasn't thinking clearly?"

"I'm just saying you walked away last time when things got too hard."

There it was. I said it. Kim left me with a litany of reasons, and Lily without explaining at all. I was terrified to see it happen again.

"And," I continued, "if we try again, the long distance would only make it easier for you to give up again."

"*I* walked away? You were always at the office when things were hard at home. You stayed late to avoid me. I *did* try to make things work during that month." Her voice cracked, her lips quivering. "But ultimately, you didn't want us to work out."

"That's not true. I wanted things to work out. That's why it hurt so badly when you left." I hesitated. "I didn't realize you saw my long hours that way."

"You blamed our whole relationship on Kim."

"What?"

"You don't remember?"

I really didn't. "No, remind me."

"I heard you talking to Kyle on the phone and telling him all the ways Kim was so different from me. I know you were still in love with her. You were just too stubborn to give up and accept we needed a divorce."

My heart stung. I had no idea she'd heard that conversation. How could I fix it?

"I wish you'd told me," I said, dropping my arms. "I was still getting over Kim, yes, but you and Kim being different wasn't a bad thing. I was vulnerable when I met you. You were probably my rebound. But wasn't I that for you as well?"

"Our whole relationship was reckless, yes. But we might have been able to make it work if you'd wanted it to."

"I *did* want it to." My heart was cracking.

"Did you seriously want us to work? Or did you" —she blinked away tears—"just not want to have to tell your family we didn't make it?"

I could hear the heartbreak in her voice, and I sat down beside her and took one of her hands. "I wanted us to work, Lily. I was in love with you." My eyes burned, tears were barely holding back.

"But what are you now?" She turned to meet my gaze.

"Now, I'm afraid. Loving someone doesn't guarantee they'll stay."

"You don't trust me."

Her eyes were filled with pain. I couldn't tell her she was wrong. "I'm sorry. I want to."

"The irony is," she said slowly, a tear spilling down her cheek. "you don't trust me now, and I left last year because I didn't trust you then. I didn't believe you really wanted me."

Her words stabbed at me like a razor-sharp blade. The truth was, I didn't trust her. I cared about her now more than I ever had before, and I couldn't stand to start something again only to have it end.

My chest was tight, like a belt was cinched around my lungs. "I know you wanted to help me, but I shouldn't have let you pretend to be my wife. It wasn't fair to either of us. My family fell in love with you this week."

"I love them too." She sniffled and swiped at her eyes. "Well, it's done now. What can we do about it?" She let go of my hand and stood up, throwing her bag over her shoulder. "I should go."

I stood and pulled her into a hug, and she wrapped her arms around me. Was this really goodbye? She was warm and soft and made my entire body ache for her. I hated this situation so much.

She pushed back and wiped her eyes with one hand and grabbed the handle of her suitcase with the other.

She focused on the floor as she rolled it to the door, and she turned back and met my eyes again as she said, "Goodbye, Joel."

My voice wouldn't work. Once she'd closed the door, I whispered, "Goodbye."

Chapter Twenty

Lily

I hurried down the hall to the elevator, determined to keep going if anyone popped out of their room to try to talk to me.

Tears burned down my face as I smashed the down arrow on the wall.

Why did I let myself get caught up in another stupid fling with Joel?

I went home and threw my suitcase and bag on the floor in the living room, then went to the bedroom and threw myself down on my bed.

I cried so hard and tried to tell myself over and over again this was for the best. Being single was best right now.

Except it wasn't.

I don't know how long I stayed in bed like that, but I fell asleep at some point and woke up at three in the morning.

I couldn't stand anything romantic at the moment, and I sighed when I turned on the TV and saw a rom com I used to love. It made me sad.

I turned the channel until I found a documentary about ancient Rome. There was nothing romantic about that, right?

I fell asleep again, and the next time I woke it was ten o'clock in the morning.

I could swear the birds chirping outside sounded tragic. Maybe there was a squirrel out there who ate all the seed again from the feeder my neighbor hung from her balcony.

I dragged myself to my little kitchen, telling myself I needed sustenance. But my freezer had no Klondike bars or anything other than frozen peas.

What the hell?

I had been eating at the hotel all week with Joel and his family and hadn't gone shopping. The grocery list I'd made before this all started was still lying on the counter.

This was an emergency. I couldn't make it to the store. I wouldn't be able to see the road through the tears that I knew would come back while I drove.

My friends didn't know the whole story. I'd have to fill them in if I wanted to talk to them about Joel leaving.

I swallowed my embarrassment and called Samantha.

When she answered, my tears came back, pouring down my face like a waterfall.

"Can I come over?" I sniffled.

"Are you okay?"

"No," I wailed.

"Maybe I should come to you. Are you at home?"

I nodded before I remembered she couldn't see me.

"Lily?" Her voice was filled with concern.

"There's no chocolate in my freezer," I wailed. "I'm an idiot."

"Hang in there, I'm coming."

She ended the call and I tossed my phone on the counter. She was at least an hour away in San Diego.

I grabbed the frozen peas out of the freezer, wrapped them in a dish towel, then held them to my aching forehead.

I don't even like peas that much. I'd been planning to make myself try eating more vegetables, but I left this one for last until it was the only thing left in my kitchen.

I turned on the living room TV and found a telenovela on. It reminded me of Joel's family too much with everyone arguing in Spanish, so I turned it to the Weather Channel.

Forty-five minutes later, my doorbell rang and I dragged myself off my couch to open the door.

Samantha was there in yoga pants and a pink sports bra. "Eliza dropped me off and she's off to get supplies."

"Did I interrupt yoga?"

She waved her hand. "I was on the way when you called, but don't worry about it."

"I'm sorry." I wiped my nose, then sniffled again.

"Don't apologize."

Samantha grabbed a tissue from the coffee table and handed it to me. I blew my nose and disgusted myself, but Samantha threw her arms around me anyway. She was a real friend.

"What happened?" she asked, rubbing my back.

"I told you, there's no chocolate in my kitchen."

She nodded and turned me around, leading me to the couch. "Eliza knows just what to get. She'll be here soon.

"How did you get here so fast?"

"Well, Eliza is a bit of a speed demon."

"No, she isn't."

"I didn't realize it either, but when she heard you were in trouble, she insisted on driving and I swear we broke the sound barrier."

How was I so lucky to have friends like this?

I hugged her again and she held me for a while, neither of us speaking.

"Do you want to talk about it?" she coaxed after a while.

"It's a long story." I sighed, sitting up straighter and wiping my nose again. "I need at least half a pack of Klondikes first."

Samantha pulled her phone out of her purse and texted Eliza. "Okay, but after Klondikes, will you tell me what's happened?"

I nodded. "As I said, it's a long story. All I have here are these frozen peas."

I pointed to the peas I left on the coffee table.

"Oh, no." Samantha kept on texting. "Don't worry, I'm on it."

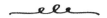

My friends sat on either side of me on my couch, both wide-eyed after I finished my story.

Samantha handed me a napkin and pointed to the side of her lips. "You've got something right here."

I cleaned the chocolate from my face and waited for my friends to react to my sordid tale.

"You can tell me what you think."

"I can't believe it." Eliza crossed her legs in her tight jeans and folded her hands over her knee. "You two seemed so perfect together. I've never seen any couple hotter on the dance floor."

"I wanted to give it a try," I said with a shrug. "I thought maybe I could travel to visit him on my breaks from work. Long distance sometimes works, right? But he didn't think so. He's too convinced that I'll leave again. Was I stupid to think we could work it out?"

"Of course not," Samantha said, rubbing my shoulder.

I leaned forward, planting my elbows on my knees and holding my face in my hands.

"I'm so sorry, Lily." Samantha tossed her long hair over her shoulder and hugged me again.

"I think I love him."

"You think?" Eliza asked as if someone had said that the sky was blue.

"Okay, I *know* I do," I said, rubbing my temples. "I wish it were enough."

"We're here for you, sweet friend," Eliza said.

"Letting me eat most of that box of Klondike bars was awesomely supportive." Although very bad for me.

Eliza put her arm around me and squeezed. She'd brought back enough food to feed me for weeks, and Samantha insisted she was going to make dinner.

I breathed in, feeling a measure of relief from getting my secrets out. I hadn't realized how much they'd weighed on me.

I knew I'd get through this somehow. My friends wouldn't let me go through it alone.

I still didn't want to leave my apartment, so I had plenty of time to mull over everything that happened.

As much as it hurt that Joel didn't trust me. I still found myself with my phone in my hands, with the text app open. I hovered my thumbs over the keyboard and asked myself again if this was a good idea.

Moving on from him might have been better, but I couldn't stop myself from wondering if we could be something. Perhaps friends? I'd rather have a piece of him than nothing at all.

Samantha had made the best butter pecan cake I'd ever tasted, and all I could think about was telling Joel about it. What was with us and this silly cake tradition? It brought a smile to my lips.

I groaned, staring at the blinking cursor on my phone waiting for me to type.

I typed out: **How's it going?**

Then I deleted it.

Next, I tried: **How was your flight?**

Delete.

I've been thinking about you.

Delete.

Could we be friends?

Delete. Delete. Delete.

I hope you made it home safely.

Screw it. Send.

Chapter Twenty-one

Joel

At my office on Monday, I couldn't concentrate on anything. The numbers and letters might as well have walked off of the page of the document I was trying to review. Nothing made sense in my life anymore.

A few of my colleagues asked me what was wrong when they saw me moping, but I couldn't tell them.

Lily was the only thing on my mind.

My phone buzzed with a text, and when I saw it was from her, my heart skipped. She was only asking if I made it home safely. What should I say? I could simply type 'yes'...but that seemed rude.

Undecided, I pushed through the workday, and still nothing made sense.

I finally pushed the papers in front of me aside and pulled out my phone to text her back:

Yes. How are you?

That was a dumb question. Delete.

I hope you're doing well.

Delete.

I put the phone down, rubbed my forehead, and growled. As I was torturing myself trying to decide what to say, and analyzing whether it was even a good idea if I responded, Lily texted again.

Lily: Samantha made a butter pecan cake with cream cheese frosting. I give it a 9.9.

Me: That's your highest score yet. Did it have nuts on top?

Lily: No, only inside. If she had put pecans on top as well, it would have been a full 10.

Me: Walnuts would make it a 10 for me.

Lily: Scandal. It's a butter PECAN cake. Bad luck. I'm sure.

I chuckled. We'd watched some re-run episodes of *The Office* in the hotel together, and I couldn't help quoting one of them.

Me: "I'm not superstitious, but I am a little stitious."

She quickly texted back with another quote.

Lily: "I just want to lie on the beach and eat hot dogs."

It made me laugh, but then I had this picture in my head of her lying on the beach in her purple bikini.

Help!

At the end of my day, I went home. I saw the green throw pillows she'd picked out, and my soul ached.

The next day, she texted again to tell me about a new song she wanted to teach her choir students in the fall and included a link.

I listened to it and agreed it would sound great with her choir. I considered asking her if she could send me a video of her students singing it when school started, but I didn't.

Sitting at home again that evening, I hated she wasn't there. It was so quiet. I put on an action movie so I could watch things blow up. Eventually, I fell asleep on her neon green pillows. They were an obnoxiously bright color, but they were so soft.

Lily texted me every day throughout the week. I barely got work done and was excited every time my phone buzzed.

I was up late every night with my mind stuck on her.

By Friday morning, I felt like a zombie. A crazy zombie with too many voices in his head. The voices said pond scum was a level above me. It was my fault she left the first time.

And the second.

I'd let my fears take over. But somehow, she still wanted to talk to me.

She wasn't really gone.

I swear I could hear every last tick of the stupid clock on my office wall. I dreaded what I had to do. It was past time for honesty. It was time to come clean. I called Tía Carmen and told her I wanted to visit Abuela for the weekend.

I booked a last-minute evening flight to Albuquerque. After work, I grabbed a few things at my apartment, then drove straight to the airport. Checking in went smoothly, but once I reached security, I came across a couple hugging and kissing goodbye.

Pushing back thoughts that wondered if that could have been me, I hurried past as fast as I could. I didn't want to risk spilling tears in the airport. I was determined I wouldn't cry.

Showing emotion like that wasn't my way. But once I got to the plane and saw an elderly man kiss his adorably wrinkled wife on her little nose, my eyes watered.

Gaaaaaaaahhhh. Forget this tough guy crap, sometimes people need to cry.

My seat was next to a young man with short, spiky blond hair with a large silver earring in his left ear. On his other side was a young woman with dark hair cut up to her jawline and feather earrings that dangled on her shoulders.

"Hi, I'm Jessa," she said, waving at me around the young man.

"I'm Joel," I said, wiping my eyes with my fingers and turning my face away. I wasn't in the mood for small talk. My stomach was twisting itself into a pretzel thinking about talking to Abuela. I needed time to mull over what I would say.

"I'm Dylan." The young man offered me his hand, knocking me on the shoulder. I felt obligated to turn to him, so I blinked back the rest of the water from my eyes and shook his hand.

Jessa leaned into Dylan and beamed. "We're on our honeymoon."

They flashed the shiny new rings on their hands at me and my stomach became painful.

Can someone turn on the sign that tells us to put our oxygen masks on now? Anything to make them stop talking to me.

My wedding ring was in my top dresser drawer. I still couldn't bring myself to get rid of it.

"Are you ready to read your poem?" Jessa asked Dylan.

"You know it, baby," Jessa said.

Oh boy. If any time would have been good for an emergency landing, it would have been right then.

Cheesy wasn't the right word. It was the worst poetry known to humankind, but neither one of them noticed.

Dylan had tears welling in his eyes as he read his "poetry". "And that's why you're cool. That's why I'm into you. Never stop being hot."

Is this guy for real?

After that, Jessa pulled him into a passionate kiss. I was convinced she could do better, but no one was asking for my opinion.

I shifted toward the aisle as much as possible in the tight seats and looked away from the incredibly uncomfortable PDA.

Okay, I royally screwed up with Lily, but at least I never tried to write her poetry.

After about half an hour, Dylan was in trouble after telling the flight attendant they didn't need anything without first consulting Jessa.

They argued the rest of the way to Albuquerque. Once the plane landed, I had a roaring headache from listening to them fight.

I couldn't wait to get out. Getting off of a plane is always agonizing, but it was even more so with the honeymooners threatening divorce behind me.

Why was love so damn complicated?

I hadn't checked a bag, so I toted my carry-on outside and called Tía Carmen. She was only five minutes away.

I got another text from Lily before I put my phone down, and I couldn't resist texting her the tale of Jessa and Dylan.

Lily: One of my students did something like that once. But he sang his poem to one of the other students.

Me: And the reaction?

Lily: She took a hard pass. And the rest of the class was impossible to settle down.

I began to type, telling her she could sing poetry to me anytime...but then I deleted it and headed outside the airport. I didn't know if I should say that.

I realized when something happened, she was the only one I wanted to talk to.

I stood on the curb waiting until Tía Carmen's little white Nissan pulled up.

When I hopped in, she said, "I know you had to work today, but there weren't any flights coming in before midnight, eh?"

"I'm sorry, Tía."

She waved that away and kissed my cheek as I clicked my seatbelt. "I'm happy you're here."

We left the airport and got onto the highway heading toward her neighborhood.

"You're always welcome here and we're so happy to have you," she said. "But you sounded so serious about spending time with your abuela. You saw her only a week ago. Is something wrong?"

"No, nothing is wrong." I wanted to keep it vague. "You know, seeing her in the hospital shook me up. None of us knows how much time we have left with her."

Tía Carmen nodded as she watched the road ahead. "See if you can talk her into getting a mammogram."

She thought that was a job for *me*?

But I had something much more uncomfortable to tell Abuela. I wanted to tell her first and everyone else later. I hadn't even called my parents to tell them I was coming into town.

When we reached the house, Abuela was asleep and it was late, so I had to wait till morning.

Tía Carmen let me sleep on the futon in her craft room. I didn't sleep much. I loved Lily more than I knew how to explain. I missed her voice, her face, and even her mess all over the bathroom. And I wanted more of those ridiculously soft neon green pillows and I didn't know where she'd bought them.

I felt lost without her.

It wasn't easy to get up after a rough night. But Abuela was delighted to have breakfast with me. Tía Carmen and Tío Pedro ate with us, and after everyone was finished, I offered to help clean up. I told Abuela I wouldn't let her help and she pretended to be annoyed with me, but I could see the amusement in her eyes.

Once the kitchen was clean, I asked Abuela if I could speak with her privately, and she suggested we go out on the back porch.

I carried her tea cup for her and helped her outside to sit on the wicker furniture that was at least as old as I was.

She sipped on her tea for a few moments while my heart was doing an impression of a greyhound being let out of the gate. Could she see me sweating?

"What is on your mind, Joel?"

I breathed in deeply and then began to lay it all out for her.

She knew about Kim turning me down, so I began by confirming I had met Lily at my friend Kyle's wedding and married her incredibly fast. But I also admitted our marriage only lasted thirty days and we divorced. I explained the rest, the fake relationship after Abuela was in the hospital, all the way up to her leaving again.

She listened quietly and waited for me to finish.

"I never meant for this to happen. And I'm so sorry for being so dishonest. Lily jumped right in and helped me when we thought you were dying."

"Joel." She gripped my hand with her tiny one and gave me a firm squeeze. "I'm disappointed you didn't feel comfortable telling me about your divorce. Marriages like that in Vegas seldom work out. I can't say I'm surprised it didn't."

"Really?" What was she saying? Wasn't she mad?

She lifted her eyebrows. "I am surprised you had enough spontaneity in you to get married so fast in the first place. You plan your entire life."

"Lily…" How could I describe what happened? "changed things for me very quickly. I fell hard. But I thought you'd be upset."

"Well, I'm not happy about this, but I appreciate that you wanted to make me happy. I admit, when I was in that hospital, I thought for a while there that I was on my way out. But how blessed I am to have a loving grandson."

Relief loosened the tension in my muscles. I'd told my story, and she wasn't crying or having palpitations. I still felt rotten, but she knew the truth now.

She studied my face. "Were my feelings about divorce really why you held back?"

"I promised my parents I wouldn't turn out like Carlos, and I always said I wouldn't."

"Well, you haven't, have you?" she asked, tilting her head to the side.

"Well, I'm divorced…" I spread my hands out with my elbows propped on my knees.

She swatted her hand to the side. "Yes, but you aren't a drug dealer." Her eyes narrowed, her face serious. "Or is there something else you need to confess?"

"What are you talking about?" I had no idea.

"Carlos got divorced because his wife found out he was selling drugs out of the back of his family minivan."

"What?"

"No one likes to talk about it." She shook her head with a solemn expression. "I'm the one who advised his poor wife to leave him."

I didn't know what to say. Was this real? Carlos was a dealer?

"I don't blame you. But you always said divorce was a dreadful sin."

She shrugged. "I admit I have evolved on a few beliefs over my one hundred years on this planet. I still believe divorce is terrible, but I don't think it's always a bad idea."

"My parents let me believe his divorce scandalized the entire family. But there was more to it all along?"

"Now hear me, Joel," she said, leaning forward and patting my knee. "Divorce may be good sometimes, but not for you."

I was confused now. "Didn't you say marriages like mine hardly ever last?"

"Yes, but when you have found the perfect woman, I expect you to make it work the second time."

"Second time? But–"

"Perhaps it was, as you say, a rebound relationship. And I agree, it's not advisable to marry so quickly." She giggled. "Except in the case of me and Abuelo. I swear I fell for him even faster than you did for Lily. Perhaps it wasn't the right time for you last year, but why isn't it now?"

She leaned back and took a sip of her tea, then set it back down on the wicker coffee table.

"I explained, Abuela. Pretending for a week was our deal, and that's all that worked for us."

Besides whatever we were right now. Friends? Text buddies?

"Ha! You certainly fooled me if you were pretending the whole time. Your abuelo used to look at me the way you look at Lily. And she seemed so enamored with you. Perhaps you're both good actors. But either way, Joel, I think you're making a mistake letting her go."

"I was afraid, Abuela."

"Perhaps she was as afraid as you. Both of you have painful pasts, but that doesn't have to mean you can't work through this together."

I wasn't doing well without her, that was for sure. I dreaded going back to Phoenix alone.

"Do you think she'd take me back after how I rejected her?"

"I will be very disappointed for you if you don't find out."

Chapter
Twenty-two
Lily

S chool hadn't started yet, and I went back to the resort in the evenings to play at the piano bar. I forced myself to do it. At first, it was agony, and I kept telling myself to stop picturing Joel out in the audience again. He was gone. Texting was all we had now.

I loved him.

I loved him in a way I'd never loved Alex.

Alex had actually texted me. It especially sucked because I'd hoped it was Joel. Why he'd kept my number was beyond my understanding. Maybe I should have changed it.

All he said at first was: **Dana dumped me.** And then: **I never should have left you.**

Wow. He finally realized that.

What should my response to that be? First I typed all the obscenities I could think of, then deleted them. I typed out several other responses but deleted each one without sending them.

Ugh.

I eventually decided to block his number. I'd only erased his number before, but this was what I should have done. He wasn't worth the effort to tell him our ship had sailed off into space and wasn't coming back. If he didn't know that already, he was irredeemably stupid.

I wasn't speaking to Dana anymore, but I'd already heard about their breakup. Dad never liked to get involved in any of our drama, so I was surprised when he mentioned it.

The resort was quiet as I walked through the doors of the lobby and went toward the stairs to the bar. All around, I saw Joel everywhere. The hall to the gift shop was on the left and the coffee shop where we'd gotten cake for our rating game. The pool area was bathed in a dim yellow and orange as the sun set below the ocean. It only reminded me of the fun we'd had out there.

I'd called my therapist again yesterday. I needed to move on and be satisfied with having Joel as a sort of friend, but I didn't know how.

The piano bar was nearly full. Only a few tables were empty. Couples sipped on drinks and listened to my colleague Andre finish his piece.

He finished up and received a lively round of applause. He was a middle-aged gentleman who always wore a gray suit.

Gray.

He took a bow, then handed the stage off to me. I took my place in front of the piano, and I played the saddest set of songs I could think of.

For my last song, I sang and played Adele's "Someone Like You". I channeled all my pain into it.

On the last verse, Chris came in to listen and took a place at one of the only empty tables near the door.

The audience was more enthusiastic than ever as I played the final notes.

I never usually bowed more than once, but this audience didn't let me go without another.

They were either huge Adele fans, or I'd done pretty well for myself this evening.

With the late hour, the manager switched to playing a jazz recording over the sound system, and I wandered over to Chris's table.

"How are you doing?" he asked.

"Fine."

Fine always means hot mess, right?

"Are you sure?" He squinted and rested his chin on his hand. "I'm told you're playing a lot of sad songs this week."

Who has a problem with that in a piano bar?

"It's called soul."

"Okay." He dropped his hand and placed it on the table. "I'm worried about you."

"Don't worry."

"Are you really okay?" He wouldn't let up.

"No. But I'm working on being okay. I was stupid to let my feelings go too far in a fake relationship."

He lifted one eyebrow. "Was it fake?"

I sighed. "I think I'll take a walk on the beach."

"You can just say you don't want to talk." He glanced down at my black pumps. "I don't feel like walking on the beach is the best idea right now."

"Mind if I leave my shoes in your office?"

He sighed. "It's the least I can do. Are you sure I can't do more? You can take more time off."

I hated the idea of being alone at my house all day. It never would have bothered me before, but missing Joel had become too intense. I needed to distract myself as much as possible. I didn't want to go back to the place where I lay in my bed and ate too many ice cream bars.

I shook my head. "I need to keep busy."

He nodded and stood. "I'll walk you out. It's against the rules to walk barefoot through the lobby."

"Even for family?"

"*Especially* for family." His eyes went wide as he said, "I don't want Aunt Margo getting any ideas."

She always took her shoes off when she came to visit, and had some kind of smelly toe fungus.

"Ew, let's just hope she never takes her shoes off again as long as we live."

He walked with me out of the bar and down the stairs. Then he held the glass door leading outside open for me. It was dark now, but the moon was full and bright.

"I can go with you," he offered as I handed him my shoes.

"I'll be fine."

I didn't stray far past the wooden boardwalk leading from the pool area to the beach. The lights around the pool weren't very bright. They were orange and pointed downward so as not to distract baby sea turtles heading for the ocean.

I used the flashlight app on my phone, but I stayed near the steps. I loved having the soft sand between my toes and breathing in and out in the fresh sea air. I closed my eyes, needing this time to relax.

"Lily?"

"Who is it?" I spun around. I didn't recognize the dim figure at first, but as it came closer I saw him. He was in the skinny jeans that drove me crazy and a black T-shirt.

"It's me, Joel." His face showed a mixture of sadness and curiosity.

My body froze. "What are you...?"

He jerked a thumb toward the resort. "Chris told me you were out here. I wanted to tell you, I went to Abuela and I confessed everything."

"Really?" My head was spinning, and my body overflowed with hope. "Is she okay?"

"Yes, she's well. I also wanted to tell you that I don't want to be afraid anymore."

An invisible vacuum sucked up all the air around me. My lungs weren't working.

"I want you in my life," he said softly. "But only if you want me."

I couldn't have been more shocked if I stood with a lightning rod on the beach in a thunderstorm. Joy and disbelief flooded my senses. His eyes were so intense I thought I might fall over.

Come up with something to say!

"I was afraid, and I let it stop me from telling you how I really felt."

"I..." I struggled, emotion nearly choking me. "I felt...like I messed up your perfectly planned life."

He blinked. "You did. But I love that you did."

I wish I had something to hold onto to hold me up.

"Lily," he continued, "no part of me wants to be single anymore. You were right. I tend to work more than I need to when there's an issue in my life I don't want to have to deal with. I'm planning to try therapy to see if I can find a better balance in my life." He took a step closer. "I don't want to be like my parents. I told you how my dad goes fishing instead of having real conversations with my mom. I didn't want to deal with my breakup with Kim, and overworking myself didn't fix anything. I think part of marrying you so quickly was me trying to run away. But that's not all it was," he quickly added. "I was smitten with you from day one and though we had issues, I was devastated when you left." He sighed and glanced down at his feet, then met my gaze again. "I'm sorry about everything."

He came even closer. "I'm still afraid, but I need to tell you why."

My throat was closing up. Was my heart still beating? How was I still standing?

"I'm afraid too," I squeaked out. Asking him to try long distance had been so difficult.

"Being without you has been torture. And in this time away from you, I've realized I love you more than I ever did before. More than I've ever loved anyone."

Tears wet my cheeks.

"We didn't do enough talking about how we were feeling," I said, finding courage from some unknown place in my body and stepping forward.

"I'm sorry I was so closed off. And I'm sorry I didn't follow you when you left last week. I hate myself for that." He breathed in deeply and released it. "Can you forgive me?"

"But..." My stomach churned and all my limbs tingled. Tears were stinging my eyes. I hoped he wouldn't notice in the weak light.

"I wish we'd taken things slower," he said softly, "and gotten to know everything about each other."

I sniffled.

Crap. Now he'll notice.

"But...where do we go from here?" I asked.

Phoenix seemed so far away, and I hated the idea of leaving my job.

"First, I'd like to look into positions here if you're okay with me living closer. Second..." He took both of my hands and squeezed gently as he sank onto one knee.

What the...

I froze in place. My eyes were probably popping out like someone watching a building crumble to the ground. Wasn't he just talking about wishing we'd taken things slowly?

The world around me was no longer steady.

"Wh-what...are you doing?" I gripped his fingers firmly and held my breath.

"Lily Rawlings, I want to know every single little thing about you. I need you in my life. Will you...date me?"

I released my breath and laughed.

"Will you date me and spend as much time as possible with me?"

I'd never heard a more amazing offer for anything in my entire life.

"Yes. Yes a thousand times. We'll go on a thousand dates, taste a thousand cakes, do a thousand puzzles, learn a thousand dances..." Okay, now I'm going overboard. I grabbed his face. "Whatever you want!"

He slipped his arms around my back and kissed me until I couldn't stand on my own anymore. I clung to him and he held me securely.

All the fear was gone. This man was everything. I'd never leave him again.

Epilogue

Lily

ONE YEAR LATER

Joel's big, crazy, wonderful Latino family had gathered again, but this time, most of them didn't have to go far. We were all in Albuquerque for Rosa's wedding.

The family church wasn't far from his parents' house, with beige stucco siding and tall stained glass windows. It even had a high steeple with an old-fashioned bell.

The wedding was lovely, and the reception hall next door was filled with white and yellow flowers and the spicy scents of a Mexican buffet.

Joel and I were seated near the head table, watching the bride and groom blush and squirm through a cheesy toast from Rosa's father, Tío Mateo.

Rosa belonged in a wedding magazine. She'd never looked so beautiful. Her off-the-shoulder dress featured a silk bodice and spread out in a full skirt with a sheer lace layer over more white silk. Rosa's new husband was a little shorter than her with a beard that nearly touched his chest. He worshiped her as if she were a goddess.

They'd met when he substituted for her a few times. I was so happy for them but more excited about what Joel might think of what I was going to do.

Her black curls were swept up in an updo so lovely, I wanted to try it for my wedding. Speaking of weddings...I'd wanted a proposal from Joel for a while. We'd decided to date for at least a year before we moved to the next step. We were determined not to go too fast this time. Now that our year was over, I decided not to wait anymore.

But I was more sure than ever he was my person.

We even went to therapy, to start over with a good foundation of trust and communication. We were both more open and honest about how we were feeling. We'd made it a year so far, working together through whatever came up.

I'd learned more about setting boundaries with my mother and sister, and I left immediately when they broke them. I didn't need to see their criticism when I moved through life. Joel still picks up after me, but now we laugh about it and both pitch in.

Joel was practicing at a law firm two miles from the resort where we fell in love again. He was religious about leaving the office at five o'clock each day. He said he couldn't stand to be at work too long when I was back in his life.

I slipped away to take care of something for my secret project, and when I came back, Joel was chatting with one of his cousins at the table with us while stealing chips off my plate.

"Hey," I said as I sat down and grabbed his hand as it was reaching over my plate. "I can't leave you alone."

"I wouldn't ever recommend that." Joel leaned over in his chair to whisper in my ear. "Where were you?" He then trailed a line of kisses from my ear to my lips.

"I had some business to take care of."

"Such as?" his eyebrows lifted and he touched his nose against mine.

"It's a secret."

It was agony, waiting for the bride's dance with her father to be over. It felt like we were living in an hourglass with a clog.

At last, it was time to throw the bouquet, and as much as I wanted to give Joel a clue of what I hoped was coming, I stepped aside to let Abuela catch it. Her face was worth it.

When it was time for the happy couple to leave, we stood outside and threw birdseed at them as they were walking to their car.

Their smiles were enormous. Rosa was beaming with joy, and I couldn't have been happier for her.

Soon they were off, and everyone wandered back inside to say their goodbyes to each other. As guests were filtering out, several members of the family remained to chat away.

Joel started talking to Abuela and I whispered in his ear, "I'll be right back."

He eyed me suspiciously but said, "Okay."

I headed to the stage. I'd found out who the DJ was from Rosa, and I'd already made a deal with him. His name was Steve, and he was such a romantic. He was an older gentleman with snow-white hair who had been married to his sweetheart for over forty years. He smiled at me and nodded, letting me know he was ready.

I snatched the posters I'd hidden behind one of the speakers and forced myself to breathe slowly and deeply.

As I gripped the microphone, my heart was bouncing like a kangaroo.

I sent Steve a thumbs up and he started the music for the karaoke version of Sara Bareilles's song, "I Choose You".

The music drew everyone's eyes to me. I faced Joel and nearly lost my nerve when our gazes locked.

I closed my eyes and started singing. The joyful upbeat melody, along with the lyrics, was so true to what was happening inside of me.

I'd seen something similar in a music video, and I hoped this wouldn't come out too embarrassing for him.

I opened my eyes and saw him smiling, then I turned my stack of posterboard around and held it up.

The first one read: **I Choose You**.

Yes, I was choosing him. Him and only him. It was now or never.

I continued to sing and Steve took the first poster from me.

The next read: **We Belong Together**.

I handed it off to Steve again, and the poster behind it read: **We Fit Perfectly**.

The next one was a drawing I'd made of puzzle pieces in all the marker colors I'd had at my apartment.

The next poster said: **I think we finally got it right.**

I paused on this one and sang the last verse of the song with all my might. Joel never took his eyes off me and walked closer to the stage. He looked amazing in that tailored, navy suit. Yes, navy. He was branching out.

Joel's abuela was openly crying with hands over her heart.

I gave the second to last poster to Steve, and the words, **MARRY ME**, were written in bold black letters and surrounded by glittery stars.

Joel grinned and rushed to the steps on the side of the stage and was by my side in seconds.

I faced him, still holding my last poster, and the words caught in my throat.

"Will...will you marry me?"

He took my poster and tossed it away, letting it flutter on the floor. He lifted both of my hands and held them to his chest. "This was my job."

"You wanted to sing me a song?" I teased.

"I'd never torture you that way." He shook his head, releasing a short laugh. "I was planning to propose to you this evening. There's a ring I've been hiding in my drawer for weeks. But if you'd rather use your grandmother's ring..."

Of course. He was such a careful planner. I should have seen this coming.

"I didn't mean to ruin your plans. I was so excited that we'd been dating for a whole year, and I..."

Wait, he was smiling. He'd bought a ring...

He lifted my chin and pressed his forehead against mine. "You beat me to it fair and square. I've never been happier than I've been this past year, and every day I can't imagine loving you more, yet, somehow it keeps happening."

I laid my palms on each side of his face. "I love you, Joel. If you marry me again, I promise I'll never–"

His lips were on mine, kissing me until I couldn't remember what I'd been trying to say. There was a vague awareness of sounds of clapping, but the world around us swiftly disappeared.

I wrapped my arms around the middle of his back and he squeezed me even closer against him.

Once we finally came up for air, I thought I should ask, "This is a yes, right?"

"I'll marry you right here and now, Lily. In another Elvis dri-ve-through if you want, or at City Hall, or with Phoenix reciting poetry, anything you want. Name it. Anytime you want."

I didn't think I would ever stop smiling. "I have nothing against Elvis, but we probably should have a *real* wedding this time without him."

"Deal." He kissed me again, sending muscle-melting warmth through my body and curling my toes.

This man was everything. I wanted to kiss him forever, and, so far, he didn't seem to mind.

Note

Thank you for reading! I'd love for you to leave a review. I'd also like to invite you to join my reader group on Facebook: Franky Brown's Rom Com Readers for news and advanced reader copies. You can also join my newsletter through my website, frankybrown.com. You can also find me on: Amazon, Facebook, and Instagram.

Also By Franky Brown

Austen Inspiration Series

Pride and Butterflies

None But You

Emma's Match

Julia's Secrets (New Adult) Series

Julia the Secret Keeper

Julia the Secret Blogger

About the Author

Franky A. Brown writes romantic comedy to make you laugh, cry and happy sigh. She holds a BA in English from the University of South Carolina and has never stopped reading. She loves bird watching, gardening, and yoga. She lives in Alabama with her husband and son.

Printed in Great Britain
by Amazon